THE ARTIST

It wants to take your pain away...

Inigo Mort

Ghostie Books

Cover design by: Jo Davies & Inigo Mort

*For the beautiful horror community, with whom I
hope to share many spooky adventures...*

ABOUT THE GHOSTIES

Royalties from 'The Artist' will be awarded to the winner of The Ghosties: An anonymous, short story horror fiction prize voted for by the community.

By supporting this novella, you are supporting indie horror authors around the world.

To find out more: www.theghostiesprize.notion.site

ABOUT THE AUTHOR

Inigo Mort lives in England with his darling wife. He is the founder of The Ghosties, an anonymous short-story horror fiction prize and dreams of opening a horror bookshop in London.

Inigo Mort reviews and rambles about horror books on TikTok and Instagram @inigohorror.

To get in touch, direct messages on social media are appreciated or email: ghosties.horror@gmail.com

TRIGGER WARNINGS

This novella is for people aged 18 and over.

Below you will find a complete list of all TW's contained in 'The Artist':

- Gore and violence
- Explicit language
- Sexual imagery and references
- Drug use and references
- Reference to suicide
- Reference to illness and death

PROLOGUE

The Artist watched the painting float face down in the lake. The canvas was soaked through, destroyed, never to be seen again. What a waste. It waded in, long thighs cutting through the water and fished the painting out. The oil bled all over its hands, and with each drop, it felt its world grow smaller.

"Goodbye..." it kissed the canvas, leaving an imprint of its teeth.

On the bank, a camcorder flashed red. The Artist didn't know what the man and woman were doing splashing around in the lake like little birds, filming themselves and listening to that noisy music. It might have left them alone if they hadn't used its painting as a prop, but it was too late now; their bodies circled each other, her blonde hair fanning like a halo, his face split in two. They would be together forever, their troubles forgotten. That was an artist's job.

"Interesting," it breathed, turning the camcorder in its hands. Times were changing. Progress.

The Artist looked back toward the old lodge, hidden among the trees. This ancient place, its home, never changed, but it had seen how fast life moved beyond the wilderness and wanted to experience it all. New people, places and ideas… it was all out there for the taking, and The Artist wouldn't stop until it had dipped its brush in all the world's blood. It couldn't bear to be trapped, treading old ground.

"I took your pain away," it said, grabbing the couple by their legs and hauling them to shore. "And now it's time to paint a new picture."

1

Drew watched the swan float upon the golden lake, autumn leaves reflected in its waters. It didn't look real; that's what he told himself to drown the feeling that he was wasting his time in New York. Places like this didn't exist. Not in real life.

His gaze drifted down the valley. Fall had burnt through the wilderness, filling the air with the smell of dead leaves. Drew could breathe easy here. There wasn't a bar of signal for miles—no pings, emails, or demands. By the end of this vacation, he'd be free of them for good.

"Heyo!"

A stone broke the water, sending the swan flapping away. Drew spun around and saw Ryan, his muscular arms raised in celebration.

"What was that for?" hissed Drew.

Ryan wrapped his arms around his friend's neck. "It's human nature to chuck stuff!" He cupped his hands around his mouth and shouted: "Echo!"

Ryan's voice died around them, swallowed up by the trees. "Huh... oh well," he said, slapping Drew's crotch. "Come check out the lodge. It's wild, you're gonna love it."

Their rental sat up the hill, its brown timber camouflaged amongst the forest. It was so well hidden that Drew couldn't see it until they stood by the SUV.

"Woah... it's big."

And it was—at least four rooms wide and three tall. Drew was impressed. The cabin was more subdued than his friend's usual tastes—penthouse suites with marble kitchens and glass rooms. He usually left the planning to them, not because he didn't care where they stayed but because Ryan never listened to him.

"Told you!" Said Ryan, basking in Drew's look of surprise. "It stinks, too."

"Of what?"

"I dunno... old stuff."

Ryan opened the door. He was right. A breath of dust and wood met Drew, smelling like no one had stayed there for years. The reception area was overwhelmingly brown—the carpets, furniture, doors, ceiling fans, and light fixtures—everything was brown except the artwork hanging on the walls.

"Guess you can never have too much landscape," said Charlotte, Ryan's girlfriend, standing by a framed picture of a sunset bleeding across a mountaintop. Ryan kissed her neck. Drew turned away.

"So, apparently, the guy who owned this place..." she began.

"Shhh!" said Ryan, widening his eyes at Charlotte. He nodded unsubtly in Drew's direction. "It's a surprise."

"Surprise?" said Drew, pretending to look at one of the cheesy paintings to distract from the knot in his stomach.

"Nothing, man. Why don't you head up and pick a room? There's only a million to choose from."

Drew would pick whichever one was furthest away from theirs.

More paintings on the first-floor landing, with three large bedrooms leading off it, each with double beds overlooking the woods. He was so used to the view from his home office, a rooftop carpark, and the Citigroup building beyond that the wilderness's open sky came as a shock.

Drew listened. Real wind, not the CPU fans that kept his triple-screen computer rig alive, and real creaking wood, the sound of the house shifting in the dirt. The world was so much more than pixels and RAM.

"This one yours?" Grey was standing in the doorway. He was so tall that he had to duck. "They're all pretty much the same. Rye and Charlotte are on the top floor, so…"

"Yeah, steer clear."

"Right," agreed Grey.

Grey was a more traditional nerd than Drew. He didn't wear expensive sneakers or eat sixty-dollar sashimi; he liked chips and Monster energy drink, which he consumed in large quantities to keep him coding through the night. He was the brains, the back end. Drew handled user experience, Charlotte marketing, and Ryan business development. Together, they made up 'Totem', a digital art trading platform that turned over $10 million a year.

"The platform's running just fine, no issues," said Grey, his long neck snaking under the door.

Drew had hoped to go just one day without hearing about work, but that's what he got for starting a business with his friends. Sometimes, he resented their success. It was sweet at first, but after he'd paid his student debts, rented a converted loft apartment, and bought all the designer bullshit his closet could hold, the taste of money had gone from green to grey. No amount of it could buy him what he truly wanted: how Charlotte looked at Ryan.

"Great, I'll check everything's AOK on my end before bed, but honestly… I'm trying to switch off," said Drew.

Grey flinched as if the idea of unplugging was an assault. Work was his safe place. Drew got that; it used to be his until he realised safe wasn't meant to feel like a prison.

Drew kicked off his shoes. "I'm going to get changed; see

you downstairs?"

Grey stared at the wall behind Drew at a painting of a lake. Something was in the water. It looked like an upside-down face.

"Did Ryan tell you yet? That Rober..."

"Bup-bup-bup-bup!" said Ryan, sneaking up behind Grey and making him jump. "Don't tell him yet!"

"Hey... hang on..." began Drew, but Ryan shoved his finger into Drew's half-open mouth, making him gag. Grey laughed at that.

"Can't anyone keep a frickin' secret around here? Wait for the big reveal," said Ryan, walking towards the stairs.

Drew changed into a hoodie and sweatpants and wandered down to the main living room. Charlotte was sitting on the edge of an uncomfortable-looking wooden couch with scratchy wool pillows. She was playing a game on her phone and jiggling her leg.

"Settling in?" said Drew.

"Hardly... this couch is pretty much slouch-proof."

Drew looked around. "I'm surprised Rye chose this place. He usually goes for something more..."

"Soulless?" She smiled, looking up from her phone.

Everyone knew Ryan was as cultured as a Vegas casino, but Charlotte still loved him. Drew didn't get it. It was Charlotte who had turned them on to art, music and books when they were young. Drew only started learning the guitar to impress her, and Ryan only clamped onto the idea of launching an NFT business because she sent him an article—that and the vast amounts of easy money to be made.

He wondered what she saw in him. Ryan was confident and exuded masculinity like strong aftershave, but Charlotte was far from 'trad wife' material. She kept her hair short, wore cat-eye specs from the fifties, Doc Martins boots, and listened to The Cure. All signs pointed to her wanting someone with blurred edges, but what you saw with Ryan was what you got. They would celebrate their fourth anniversary in the Bahamas that Christmas.

Drew flopped down beside her and almost broke his tailbone on the upholstery. Charlotte laughed.

"Mom would have an anurism if she saw how this place was decorated."

"She okay?" said Drew.

Charlotte shrugged. "The same. Busy." A cloud passed over her face.

"So... what's this secret that Rye keeps going on about... or not going on about?" said Drew.

Charlotte shook her head but didn't offer anything up.

"It's not a prank, is it?" he said, trying to mask the vulnerability in his voice.

"Don't worry. It's kinda cute, actually, in a weird sort of way... cute by Rye's standards."

Drew was about to comment when he noticed something red smeared on the back of Charlotte's top. It looked like blood. "Oh shoot... I think you've cut yourself."

"What?" she said, following his eyes.

"Here... let me."

She flinched when he reached out. "Sorry... PMDD bullshit. Sensitive skin." She dipped his fingers beneath her top and stretched out the fabric. It was too vibrant and sticky to be dried blood. She sniffed it.

"Paint?" he said, eyeing her bare skin.

Charlotte frowned and peeled some of it off. "Acrylic," she agreed. "Where the f..."

Ryan was in the doorway watching them. "You two lovebirds having fun?"

Drew's heart fell apart. Ryan loved making things awkward. It was perverse.

"There's wet paint somewhere in the house," Drew said, standing up.

"Unlikely," snorted Ryan. "This place has had less TLC than my gam-gam, and she's been dead for ten years."

"One of the paintings, maybe?" offered Drew, but that was stupid; they were all clearly from the '80s, in that creepy naive style with too many colours and not enough shading.

"I'm gonna change," said Charlotte.

"You do that, then..." clapped Ryan, "We should get this party started!" He dug into his pocket and pulled out a clear plastic baggie filled with white powder.

Drew groaned.

"No, no, you're not getting out of it this time!" Ryan wagged his finger.

"I told you, it makes me feel like ass afterwards. I'm here to chill, not rot in bed for a week," said Drew.

Ryan shook the bag in his friend's face, eyes sparkling.

"Don't be a dick," said Charlotte as she walked past him. "If he says he doesn't want it, he doesn't want it."

"Fine! More for me," said Ryan.

Drew's party days were behind him, but Ryan and Charlotte still liked to get wasted on weekends. Ryan was a pusher when it came to drugs; he didn't like doing them alone. Unlike Drew, Ryan had always been good at ignoring the murky stuff that drove the urges. That's what kept him young at heart: he was pathologically unable to take any responsibility.

"Set me one up..." shouted Charlotte from the stairs. She was self-aware enough to know she was self-medicating, exorcising her demons for the night, but that didn't make her any wiser than Ryan. If anything, Drew found her drug use even more depressing.

"Shall we adjourn to the pantry?" said Ryan, twiddling an invisible moustache. He liked to imitate Drew's English accent.

"The pantry?"

"Oh, you know, the dining room, or whatever you posh British folk call it."

"What's got you so excited?" said Drew, narrowing his

eyes.

Ryan grinned roguishly. "Oh, you'll see."

The dining room was large, with a rustic wooden table running its length. Although it was still light outside, someone had drawn the curtains and lit candles, which dribbled red wax down their holders. The walls flickered and wobbled.

Ryan approached the table and began dumping white powder onto a plate. "Drinks!" He ordered, snapping his fingers at several bottles of wine that Charlotte had left on top of a mahogany chest of drawers. While Drew hunted for a corkscrew, Ryan rolled up a note.

"So… you're probably wondering…" *Snort* Ryan closed his eyes and shuddered. "What all the mystery is about." He rubbed his gums. "Frick that's tasty…" He blinked with a dumb grin.

Drew sighed and started pouring the wine.

"Notice anything… strange about this room?" said Ryan.

Drew looked around. The whole house was pretty strange, but in this room, nothing jumped out besides the unnecessarily long table. "I mean, the walls aren't crammed with those ugly landscapes."

Ryan ripped up another line of white powder and coughed. "No?"

"Um…" And then he saw it: a shadow, something hiding in the far corner of the room. It was taller than Drew and covered in a black sheet. "What is it?" he said, walking towards it.

"Bup-bup-bup!" Ryan held Drew's shoulders. "Charlotte! Grey!" he yelled. "It's time!"

Ryan was already starting to get under Drew's skin, but he didn't want to start bickering with him this early into the trip. Hopefully, he would burn himself out on the first night and leave Drew in peace for the remainder of the vacation.

Grey walked in first, balancing his laptop on one of his

long, white forearms. "Good news, I've set up the router and scheduled the Madwire update for 09:00 AM Eastern time. Should massively cut down the latency on the..."

"Greyshutthefuckup!" said Ryan, taking the laptop off him and closing the lid. "Big brain time is over. Small brain time now..." He pointed at the mound of cocaine.

Grey ignored him and picked up the laptop again. Charlotte followed shortly. She had added some black wings to the corners of her eyes.

"You look good," smiled Drew.

"Thanks, hun," she said, then, "don't mind if I do," taking the rolled-up twenty Ryan held out. Ryan looked at Drew as if to say, 'I know what she really wants, and it ain't you.' Drew knew that wasn't what he meant; it was just that the cocaine had set his jaw hard, and he looked meaner. Drew cringed at himself. He wasn't entitled to Charlotte and was happy she was with his oldest friend, but that didn't mean he could easily crush those ancient feelings.

Ryan drumrolled on the table, making the candlelight dance. "Are we all here? Are we all... ready?"

"Jesus Christ, Rye," said Drew. "This better be good."

"Oh... it is." Ryan strutted to the corner of the room where the shadow stood against the wall and rested his hand on the sheet. "Now..." his eyes swept the room. "We've had a good year, scratch that, an insane year. Charlotte and I wanted to plan something truly memorable... something that resonated. A personal touch, to show you we care."

Drew didn't understand why Ryan was staring at him.

"Grey couldn't give two shits about where we go on vacation as long as there's wifi, but as for our glorious UX genius, Drew... I know he likes to think of himself as a... man of culture." Ryan tugged on the black sheet covering the shape, just enough to make it crease into a smile.

"So I thought, why not take him somewhere meaningful, with a bit of history, somewhere transporting..."

"Rye..." Drew sighed.

He held his hand up. "My mum always used to say... Xīngxīng zhī huǒ, kěyǐ liáoyuán. Starlight shines far. It means small actions have far-reaching consequences."

Drew turned to Charlotte and raised his eyebrows. She laughed. Ryan was anything but a philosopher, but seeing he'd given this speech some thought was touching.

"I knew you'd like that," winked Ryan, "but the point is, if it weren't for you and Charlotte being such little art nerds, then Grey would still be fapping into a sock and I... well, I would still be just as rich and handsome."

Charlotte hooted.

"No, seriously, I'm too much of a smooth-brained idiot to have thought of starting Totem. I wouldn't know good art if Picasso painted it on my eyeballs. It's all down to you guys... and a little someone called... Robert Frost, where it all began."

Ryan stared at Drew with a wide grin as if he expected him to react. Drew looked back blankly. "I'm sorry... who?"

"Charlotte?" Ryan's tone was accusatory.

"Oh, you know, Robert Frost..." said Charlotte, turning to Drew. "The guy on TV who did those 'how-to-paint' things. Big hair? Yellow teeth?"

Drew nodded. Now he remembered. "The guy we used to watch at breakfast after sleepovers?"

Ryan rubbed his face in exasperation. "For... frick sake, Charlotte, you said Robert Frost was one of Drew's heroes. We could be in Miami right now!"

Charlotte crinkled her face up. "No, I didn't! I said he used to like watching his show. And he liked his big hair. You remember, right?" She grinned manically at Drew.

Drew only sat through those shows because it meant spending precious quiet moments with Charlotte—the fact she had remembered filled his heart. "Yeah, of course... ol' Robbert Frost. The guy who used to paint with ketchup."

Ryan was shaking his head and grinding his teeth.

"Jesus Christ, well... now I look like a madman."

"No... not at all. This is ridiculous and... thoughtful? And I love it," said Drew. "Whatever happened to that Frost guy anyway?"

The light returned to Ryan's eyes. "I'm glad you asked... in fact, that you don't know will make this a thousand times better." He turned and looked up at the black shape behind him. "So... Robert Frost was big in the eighties. Everyone loved him. He was, like, as family-coded as it gets. Super blissed-out, peace and love, wholesome crap. His paintings were nasty, even I know that, but his skill was that he was a great communicator; he made you feel like you could paint just like him, that anything was possible, from old ladies to kids. That was his brand."

Drew remembered sitting at Charlotte's parents' kitchen island, watching Robert Frost paint mountains with toothbrushes on her fuzzy TV box. He could picture her resting on her elbow, a spoonful of cereal raised halfway to her mouth, totally entranced. Even then, Drew chased that look she gave Robert Frost, the same look she now gave Ryan.

"He was a legend who stole the breakfast-eating nation's heart, a legend who, in the autumn of... 1995, vanished from the face of the earth."

"Wait... what?" Said Grey, who, up until now, had still been typing.

"Yeah... what are you talking about?" Said Drew. "What do you mean Robert Frost vanished?"

"Poof!" Ryan shimmered his fingers. "Without a trace."

Drew flicked the underside of his chin. "How did I not know that?"

"I dunno... No social media in the 90s? It was a whole thing; they even made a documentary about it a few years back on 'Unsolved', but it's a bit of an anticlimax because no one knows where Frost went."

"Unsolved... clues in the name," said Grey.

Ryan waved him away. "He just... renounced all his worldly possessions and... walked out into the wilderness."

"So... did he die? Did get beamed up?" Drew turned to Charlotte, who nodded to confirm her boyfriend's story.

Ryan shrugged. "I have no idea... but I haven't got to the best part yet." He gripped the black sheet. "Before Frost vanished, he did one final painting..."

"Wait... Wait..." Drew cocked his head. "We're not... this isn't?"

"You bet! We are standing in Robert Frost's wilderness lodge, the last place he was seen... alive." With that, Ryan pulled on the black cloth, which slipped to reveal a portrait of a naked figure surrounded by darkness. "And this is his magnum ocus!"

"Magnum opus," corrected Charlotte.

Drew took a step towards it. "What the..." This was nothing like the landscapes Frost painted on TV. The figure was scratched and blurry, head thrown back and arms spread. "It looks hellish..."

"And what about that raw-ass dong?" said Ryan, pointing to what looked like a bloodied penis tucked between the figure's thighs. "Too much of the old..." he shook his wrist making a rusty-gate noise.

"This can't be real..." murmured Drew.

"This was the last piece he ever painted. And then... poof... into the creek. If you believe the nuts online, sounds like he had some sort of vision. Tomorrow morning, we'll walk down past the lake and see if we can't find the ol' freak ourselves."

"You're messing with me," Drew said.

Charlotte shook her head. "No, it's legit. We found his lodge on some crusty rental site that looked like it hadn't been updated in... forever. I called the trustee, thinking it was a joke, and this old woman, his cousin, owns it. He didn't have any other family. I don't think she'd ever heard of AirBnB."

"Wait... so you just randomly stumbled on this place?" Drew wasn't convinced.

"Pretty much. I was looking for forest retreats out west, and this was, like, on the third results page." Grey walked up to the painting and stared at it. "I don't like it."

The subject's face was scarred with paintbrush strokes, like Frost was trying to score out its features.

"Yeah, it's horrendous," said Ryan, walking to the table and coiling a banknote.

Drew hadn't consciously realised that he'd taken two steps back from the painting and was now standing on top of Charlotte. She poked him in the ribs, making him jump. "I don't buy it," he said. "Frost's lodge... this lodge... shouldn't it be famous?"

Ryan did a line. "Well, it's a good thing it isn't, because it was an absolute steal. Only $90 a night. I think the cousin is still operating on 1980s inflation."

"$90 a night?" Drew scratched his head. "For this whole place? There are like eight rooms. Don't you think that's a bit... cheap?"

Ryan sauntered between Drew and Charlotte, carrying two glasses of red wine. "Her loss. Now, let's toast to good ol' Robert Frost. I hope he packed an extra layer or two because fall nights get cold all the way out here."

"Guess there is something to be said for worldly possessions," said Charlotte, gulping.

"I'll drink to that."

2

The rest of the evening went predictably. Grey went the distance with Ryan and Charlotte, tapping away on his keyboard while they talked earnestly about everything and nothing, their words becoming more slurred with each chime of the grandfather clock. The wine started closing Drew's eyelids at midnight, and he excused himself.

Before he left, he turned to Frost's painting and gave it a diplomatic nod, making peace with it. The splayed, featureless body wasn't the TV personality's usual style, and the fact it was supposedly his final work irked Drew.

The forest was impossibly dark outside, a solid thing. Drew squinted through his bedroom window, suddenly missing the reassuring sound of New York's car horns and sirens. The trees, the creek, and the black sky held them now, except those things wouldn't come running if something went wrong.

Drew slipped under the cold sheets and took out his phone, feeling reluctantly thankful for Grey's router. He typed 'Robert Frost', 'Disappeared' and 'Vision' into Google.

The first few results confirmed Ryan's story: a YouTube video featuring a conspiracy neckbeard, which he skipped after a minute, a Netflix piece promoting their Unsolved episode, and a backdated article in the Times. Information pre-internet was hard to come by, but Drew kept scrolling until he found an interview Frost had done with an Art Magazine called *Splash*, uploaded as a scanned PDF file.

After the phenomenal success of EASY AS PIY (Paint It Yourself), how easy is it to stay motivated?

I'd be in my garden shed painting, rich or poor, blue skies or grey. My wife sometimes jokes that I wouldn't know if it was the end of the world... Art isn't about making money; it's about bringing people together and making them forget their troubles. Failing that... putting a smile on their faces. I'll die with a paintbrush in my hand.

You have famously never exhibited your work; why is that?

I don't know about famously... but that's true. I know that my paintings aren't high art. That's the point. They're supposed to be accessible, and for me, as soon as you put a value on art, you're kinda saying, 'It's too good for the likes of you.'

Your paintings aren't for sale?

So, here's the thing: My job is to get other people to paint; it's not about me. If your painting doesn't look identical or better than mine after watching one of my shows, then I've not done my job, and NBC should fire me. Great art... nature's art... is free. All I do is capture it, but that doesn't give me the right to sell it. I'm not here to colonise. So, no, I'll never sell any of my work.

That's interesting. Could you expand on what you mean by colonising?

Capitalism is the biggest evil in the world. I spend a lot of time in nature, and let me tell you, at this rate, in fifty years, it'll all be gone. I try as hard as I can to counterbalance the harm done by my paymasters at NBC; I live off the land and get out of the city as often as possible. Some people will call me a hypocrite, but that's okay. It's not my fault I was born into this system, and one day, I hope to leave it... for good. Until that day, I will never sell my work to people with more money than sense. If you've got enough money to buy expensive art, you don't deserve it.

So, is it... over your dead body?

Not even then, if I can help it.

Drew dropped his phone into his lap, imagining what Robert Frost would have thought about four ultra-capitalists sleeping in his house. Not just any ultra-capitalists; server-farming, bitcoin-mining, blockchain-inscribing, art-tokenising capitalists. It was a cold fact that cryptocurrency was responsible for producing as much CO_2 per year as all the world's homes combined. Drew had told himself that at least he wasn't working for an arms or oil firm. That wasn't saying much, but a regular job wouldn't pay the rent on his $6000-a-month apartment in New York, and no one got rich from doing anything good. Apart from Robert Frost, apparently.

'*It's not my fault I was born into this system, and one day, I hope to leave it... for good.*' It seemed that Frost's wish had come true. "You and me both," he whispered to himself.

Drew heard Ryan and Charlotte stumbling to their room, their footsteps thumping through the ceiling, followed by giggling. They'd probably run out of drugs and were looking for their next fix, and he knew what that meant. Sometimes, he couldn't help himself: Ryan's low moans and Charlotte's breathy cries. He knew it was wrong to listen, but it wasn't like he was sneaking around outside their door. Their noises sought him out, and he let them in. Part of him desired them both, but shame rode the back of that desire. He didn't want to feel those things tonight, so he put in his earbuds and played a podcast.

The following morning, Drew woke up feeling hungover. The dining room was a mess: empty wine bottles, plastic cups, greasy smudges of powder, and the onion smell of sweat. He'd bank some passive-aggression points and tidy up after them.

Frost's painting glared at him as he moved through the wreckage with his trash bag. He stopped and threw the cover over it, which made him feel better, but he still imagined it watching him through the threads.

When it was done, surfaces wiped, and bottles recycled, he made himself a coffee and walked onto the porch. The air was crisp, and a grey sun flashed through the trees. It reminded him of when his parents took him camping in Finger Lakes as a kid, rising early to fry streaky bacon and eggs. Coming from the city, it felt like they were the only ones left in the world. Dad was always working, and sometimes Drew wished Mum worked too so she would stop fussing, but those trips were the rare times that everything felt evened out, all of them together, with nowhere to be. He missed them both so much.

"Cheers," he said, raising his coffee to them. Dad always said that before he drank, whether it was tea, coffee, beer or, occasionally, soup.

"Morning," came a crumpled voice. It was Charlotte.

"Morning. You're up early, considering."

"I never get more than six hours after partying." She sat on the porch and stared into the woods, eyes glazed. Drew knew she would be hurting and didn't want to hear her pretend otherwise, so he let the sound of the trees fill the space between them.

Charlotte stared down at a pair of pills nestled in her palm and then dry swallowed them.

"Bad headache?" he said.

She paused. "Something like that." She ran her fingers over her ribs.

Together, they watched a plump little robin hop amongst the leaves, half a worm hanging from its beak. Drew knew they were both thinking the same thing: sometimes, being a human was shit.

"You said you wanted to go explore the creek after breakfast?"

"Hunting for Raw-Dong?"

"Raw-Dong?" said Drew.

"Frost's self-portrait. You know…" she said, stretching her arms wide and tipping her head back.

"You think that's a self-portrait of Frost?" he said.

Charlotte shrugged. "I mean… depending on how…" she spun her fingers around her head "… simple you are, it could be his final vision… the one that made him walk off into the wilderness," she smirked. "Total crap."

Drew felt a chill skuttle up his spine. "Do you reckon Ryan will want to come?" He said, holding his breath.

"Doubt it. You know what he's like. He'll sleep all day and be ready to do it again tonight."

Drew heard something tinging her voice, not just tiredness, but hollowness. Dating Ryan was a drug in itself. When his attention was focused on someone, they felt invincible; when it was gone, he left them drained. Ryan fed on the energy of those around him. He relied on Grey to build his dream business, Charlotte to love him, and Drew to make him feel tall. Drew was used to Ryan's teasing, but that didn't mean he liked it.

"What did you get up to last night?"

"Oh, you know…" she trailed off. "Dumb shit."

"What time did Grey get to bed?"

Charlotte hesitated, and for a terrifying second, Drew imagined her confessing that the three of them, Ryan, Grey and Charlotte, had had a threesome. He didn't know why he thought that, but he felt jealousy crackle inside him.

"He was up after we went to sleep."

"Doing what? Working?"

She nodded, but Drew could tell there was more to it.

"So I guess it'll be just the two of us," he said.

She took his hand and squeezed it but said nothing.

"I'll make you breakfast. What do you fancy?"

"No, you don't need to…"

"No problem, you're on vacation, and I never have anyone to cook for. Bacon and eggs?"

She smiled weakly and nodded. That made Drew feel good. He'd make Charlotte a beautiful breakfast while Ryan snored and farted in bed. "Coffee with almond milk, right?"

"Right."

"You stay here and chill; I'll be back in fifteen. Want a blanket?"

Charlotte kept on staring straight ahead.

"Charlotte?"

When she turned to him, her eyes were glistening. "No. Thanks, I'm fine."

Drew watched the bacon and eggs bubbling in the pan, trying to find the courage to come clean. He had planned to wait until the end of their stay to avoid any collateral awkwardness, from Ryan in particular, but he didn't like lying to Charlotte. He'd wait until they were alone in the wilderness before bringing it up. Maybe she'd agree to keep it between them until he found the nerve, but there was no telling what might happen if she felt angry or hurt once he confessed.

"Bread fried in dripping, scrambled egg, charred bacon with a drizzle of maple syrup and a piping-hot cup of wake the heck up," he smiled, handing her the plate.

"Looks delish," she said, putting it beside her and focusing on the coffee.

Drew sat down. "I read about Robert Frost last night. Brought back a lot of memories. Of the good old days. Me and you... watching him."

The steam from the coffee enveloped her face.

"Time moves fast. Who'd have thunk we'd have ended up here?" he continued, despite her silence. "I remember one night, Halloween I think, when your mum went out to one of her city functions and left us with $50 for pizza and movies. It was like we'd won the lottery. We were balling. And we managed to convince the Blockbuster guy to rent... oh, what was it? I can't remember.... Something gnarly and way too scary for us at twelve. I remember sitting, swallowed up in your mum's massive couch, the one that vibrated, stuffing myself with pizza and Doctor Pepper, scared shitless, but thinking... man, this is the only life I ever wanted to live."

He looked at her just as the sunlight caught the tip of her nose. "Now, look at us. We've got more than we ever wanted, but damn, it doesn't feel like it. Was it just because we were young? No responsibilities? No bills? No tax? I'm not so sure. I was anxious all the time when I was young. Stressed with school, making friends, and when mum, and then dad... no. I think it's because, back then, we took the time to just... be. We grabbed the quiet moments, and they seemed to last for years."

Charlotte picked up a rasher of bacon and turned it slowly, the sunlight filtering through the fat and sinew. "The Evil Dead 2."

"What?"

"That's the movie we rented," she said, taking a bite and putting the rest back on her plate.

"Right," he nodded. "Fuckin'... Bruce Campbell. He was so cool." A warm feeling melted through his chest. She remembered, too, he thought. "But yeah. This interview with Frost... turns out he was, I dunno, a socialist, or a pagan or something. He would have fucking hated us," he laughed.

Charlotte usually had a sense of humour, but the comedown must have hit her particularly hard that morning. She just stared at the fallen leaves.

"Are you okay?" he said, putting his arm around her.

"Nah, not really."

"Oh?" He felt a spike of adrenaline. "Want to talk about it?"

"I don't know." She wiped her nose with her sleeve and sniffed twice. "Maybe in a bit... sorry, I need to snap out of it."

"Yeah, well, like you said, maybe a walk to clear your head? After you've eaten." His eyes fell on the still-full plate of food.

"Sorry, Drew, my appetite's gone. But it looks delicious. Thank you."

"No, of course," he said, feeling like an idiot but not knowing why. "And the walk? Too tired?"

"Nah, let's do it. Get the blood... flowing," she smiled, and it was like the sun turned gold.

3

Once Charlotte was dressed, they headed out into the woods. The swan was gone from the lake, but the wind had shaken a layer of yellow leaves onto its surface, making it indistinguishable from the path. They skirted the banks and continued into unknown territory, emerging into a clearing overlooking a vista that smouldered orange. Cutting through the trees, a boulder-lined creek snaked onto an open plane.

"Wow. It's beautiful," said Charlotte. "In a… sad kinda way."

Drew thought that could mean a hundred things: sad that the trees looked like skeletons, sad that the sun was trapped behind the clouds, sad that their lives were so apart from this wilderness.

"I always find big things sad," she continued. "They're so… lonely."

"I was about to say peaceful. Guess that says something about me." Drew spent a lot of time on his own, talking to people through a screen. Some days, the only skin he saw was the delivery riders', and even they were hidden behind bike helmets. That would all change soon. If it didn't, the circle of ice that made up his life would melt, and he didn't know how long he'd be able to tread water. "I've been meaning to..."

"Oh! Look!" burst Charlotte, pointing down the creek to a rocky platform. "That view is insane."

Drew swallowed his confession and stumbled after her. The rocks were slippery, and the water splashing the toes of his trainers was freezing. He didn't want to fall and make a fool of himself in front of Charlotte. She wouldn't poke fun at him like Ryan, who would almost certainly have pretended to help him up before pushing him back into the water, but what he needed to say next had no space for chattering teeth and blue lips.

They arrived at the platform, a pool of rainwater forming a shallow bird bath in its centre. The view was even more spectacular from here, the trees warping into the sky as the creek disappeared over the horizon. Charlotte took out her phone and held it up. "Hey, quick, selfie," she said, pulling him close and smiling widely. Drew didn't like photos; he never knew what to do with himself.

"Aww, cute!" she said, shoving the phone in his face to show him the shot. Drew smiled tight-lipped. He thought he looked like a plank. "You look great," he said.

"Hey, how fuckin' scary would it be if we saw Frost wandering around in the creek... or... in the back of the photo..." she said, shaking his arm. "What do you think? Reckon he's out here somewhere?"

"Nah... he'd never have survived. Missing persons cases rarely end well."

"Yeah, it's... what did your dad always say? *Bollocks*," she said in an English accent. "He's dead for sure."

Drew didn't like thinking about dead people and his dad, alone and cold in the ground. He had a very British sense of humour: On his tombstone, he told the mason to carve the phrase 'I buried the gold in the...'. Everyone laughed at the funeral, but not Drew.

"How are you... feeling about all that?" she said.

"By 'all that' do you mean... my dad being dead?"

She looked mortified. "Oh shit... no."

"Just messing with you. Yeah... sometimes it feels big... other times it feels small. But it never goes."

"He's always with you?"

"They both are," he nodded.

Charlotte dipped her toe in the water. "This is gonna sound bad... but sometimes I think I'll love my Mom more after she's... dead."

Drew raised an eyebrow. "Yeah... that does sound bad."

"Not like that. I just mean... she can be suffocating. Like... I don't know..."

"Like you need some distance?"

"To know how I feel... yeah. She doesn't leave me much room to make that choice. She dominates, you know?

"I can see that. No offence," said Drew.

"I just wished she'd loosen up. Smoke a blunt or something."

"Frost seemed like he might be partial to a bit of weed. Maybe even LSD," he offered.

"Yeah... well, not that far." Her gaze drifted up towards the stony sky yawning overhead.

Drew wondered what it would feel like to lose touch with reality. Not in the way he already had, slowly cutting himself off from the world, but more... seeing things that weren't there. As a guilty onlooker of the alt-right pipeline, crypto bros and basement dwellers, he knew a thing about conspiracy theories and how their explanations for a messed-up world were so seductive. They were truth's shadow, a glimpse of something murky that appealed to the worst in people.

"He did come across a bit funky in the interview I read. He talked about wanting to live off the land. Maybe he picked the wrong mushroom."

"God, taking mushrooms here would be epic," she said, snapping another photo.

Drew gazed into the pool, watching her reflection.

"I wonder if Frost had a wife? What happened to her?" Charlotte stared off.

"I know zero about any of it," said Drew. "But... you'd kinda assume she left him or something... he must have been a total weirdo."

He watched Charlotte's face ripple as the wind stroked the water. She looked sad again.

"Yeah... probably."

If he didn't say what was on his mind soon, he might miss his window. His life was not going to plan, but when the enablers of his depression were also his childhood friends, it made things tricky. He needed to be delicate, to let her know it wasn't them; it was him. "Okay, if I don't say this now, I might..."

"I know what you're going to say."

Drew looked up at her, fear stinging him, wondering how she could possibly know he wanted out of Totem, the business they had built together. He'd never been good at hiding his true feelings, but he'd put in extra effort for this final trip: a brave face. If Charlotte knew, then so did...

"Rye and I... It's not working out." She sat down on a rock, holding her head.

"What?" Fear and hope bubbled in him like oil and water, repelling each other. "No... I didn't..."

"No point hiding it... a kid could see it's not working. It's getting... toxic."

Drew knelt at her feet.

"He's changed but... I don't want to change him; he's great as he is..."

Drew nodded a little too vigorously.

"He's not in touch. He hides from himself... from me. And the drugs... shit, the drugs... they're bandaids that have stopped sticking." Her arms fell to her side, her face streaked with tears. "I've been trying to work out how to tell him. He's like a brother to me... wait, that sounds wrong. I mean, he's one of my oldest friends. Like, our folks go out on double dates."

Drew took her hands. They were cold and shaking.

"Where I'm headed... is not good. I'm burnt out, and if I don't course-correct soon, I will end up..." Her skin creased, and she let out a sob that echoed around the creek and Drew's heart. "I just... don't know... how..." her words were drowning, wave after wave of tears knocking them back down her throat.

Drew stroked her arms, feeling his eyes bite. "Listen. You had a heavy night; you're exhausted. I'm not saying these feelings aren't real... you're right; I have seen it. But what are you going to do? Do you want to deal with it now? On this trip?"

The emotions Drew felt were overwhelming. His oldest friend, the girl he had loved since he was ten, was breaking apart in his arms, telling him what he had wanted to hear for so long, a thing which made him hate himself: that she didn't want to be with Ryan anymore. Not only that, her confession overshadowed his. He wondered what Ryan would do if his girlfriend and best friend abandoned him on the same weekend. It would be the end of everything: the business, the gang of four, all gone.

"I know, I know." She sniffed. "But... there's never gonna be a right time. And... oh fucking christ... that's not even the worst part." Her hand drifted down to her stomach.

Drew didn't like the way she said that. "What? What do you mean?"

Her mouth flew around her face as if possessed. "I... oh, don't hate me, please. Don't think I'm bad for not telling you..."

"Tell me." His heart thumped. "Listen, look at me." She did, through her fringe, her eyes red. "I can help you through anything. I can be a sounding board for everything: your fears… whatever's holding you back."

Charlotte inhaled sharply, her eyeballs back sucked into her head. "What is that?" She pointed a shaking finger over his shoulder.

Drew spun around and saw a shadow sneaking back through the rocks. He jumped up, chest heaving. "Ryan? Grey?" He turned back to Charlotte, her mouth stretched open in fear. "What was it?"

A snot bubble burst from her nose.

"Was it an animal?" Drew had read about Black Bears living in the northern region, but he knew they were shy and kept themselves away from humans. He took a step towards the rocks, but Charlotte grabbed his arm.

"No… don't." Her eyes darted around the creek, and then she said, "Drew, I don't like it."

He turned up the creek. "Hey! Asshole! Fuck off!" His voice shook. A thought crept into his head, but he brushed it off, suppressing a nervous laugh. There was no way. Robert Frost was either dead or in the Argentinian jungle painting waterfalls. "Look, I think… and I don't want to be a dick, but you're having a bad reaction to whatever that shit was cut with last night, and… the stress. I think you're right; we do need to get back."

"You didn't see it?"

"No, no, I didn't. I saw… the sun hitting the rocks. I didn't see anything."

Her eyes were fixed on the spot behind them.

"Oh… come on." He said, pulling her up. "Whatever it was, it's gone."

"Fuck… maybe I am going crazy…" she said, falling into his arms.

Drew felt his heart double in weight, but he stroked her hair, rocked her, and told her that everything was okay and that she was safe. Charlotte was going through something profound and traumatic, and suddenly, his problems seemed like the pebbles in the creek, smooth and small amongst jagged boulders. "Here's what we're going to do. We'll get back to the lodge, run you a hot bath, and I'm gonna get Grey to find out what kind of animals we've got out here... I reckon you could have seen a wolf or a deer or... I don't know. There's always an explanation. Always."

She nodded gently into his chest. Her breathing was slowing; she was coming back to him. "Yeah... I mean, my eyes were full of tears. Probably just got all distorted. And I'm not wearing my glasses, so yeah..."

"I'm not saying you're lying." Drew turned to lead her up the rocks, but she stayed put.

"Drew? We keep what I said between us, yeah? Just between us."

Drew nodded reassuringly. "Of course. But... what about the thing... you said there was more."

She bit her lip. "Oh... later, I promise. I think... I need a rest."

"Of course, take your time. I'm here for you. And as for the Ryan stuff... I mean, if I were you, I'd wait until we were back in New York. This is heavy shit, and neither you nor Rye wants to be trapped out here trying to figure it out. Agreed?"

"I think you're right."

"Good. Then, let's go. My feet are blocks of ice."

They tramped through the woods, Charlotte two paces ahead. She was rattled, and he couldn't blame her for that. He hoped she could keep it together before the whole thing blew up. "I'm going to run you a bath. I'll make you some tea. You haven't eaten anything. No wonder you..."

Something cracked through the undergrowth. Charlotte wailed, and Drew froze as a shape loomed into view. "Oh shit..."

"What? Where?"

"Look!" whispered Drew. His eyes were sparkling. "Look!"

A white deer, its coat yellowed with grease, watched

them from the tree line with jet-black eyes. One of its antlers had snapped off, and the other was tangled with leafy twigs.

"Oh my god," she said, squeezing Drew.

"See! I told you." Relief soaked through them both.

"Thank fuck. I thought I was going crazy. For real."

They both laughed and stared as the white deer sloped away, its head bobbing up and down.

"What's it doing up here alone?" She pulled out her phone.

"No idea. But who cares? That's definitely what you saw. Those eyes... bit creepy," he chuckled. "It didn't look very well, did it?"

"No," agreed Charlotte. "Maybe it lost its herd."

"Yeah. Well, I hope it's okay," he said quietly. "Come on, let's get back and tell the others."

"Wait..." said Charlotte, taking out her phone and snapping a picture of the white deer as it walked away. "An alibi."

Drew smiled, but he wondered what she meant. He hadn't realised they'd need one.

4

When they returned to the lodge, they found Ryan spread across the couch, one hand gripping his phone and another down his boxers. Drew was conscious that he needed to act normal, but normality suddenly felt abstract, like the fast-fading memory of a dream. He nodded at Charlotte to head upstairs before sitting down beside Ryan. "You all good?"

"Frickin' fantastic," he said without looking up. "Where have you two lovebirds been?"

Drew clenched his jaw. "Bro… don't call us that. It's weird."

Ryan looked Drew dead in the eyes and smiled. He loved messing with Drew and always had since they were kids. It was his way of proving the strength of their bond; no amount of teasing could break them apart. At the junior prom, Ryan poured a cup of diet coke down the front of Drew's suit pants, and for the rest of the senior year, everyone called him 'Drewpee'. It wasn't a nickname that scored him any points with the girls in his year, and it followed him to college like a bad stink. Charlotte had encouraged him to confront Ryan about his behaviour, but Drew shrugged it off. Pick at that scab after all those years of teasing, and their relationship might bleed out.

"Seriously, what were you up to?"

"We went down to the creek."

Ryan raised his eyebrows. "Oh… did you see anything spooky?"

"We saw a white deer."

"Oh, what? That's pretty sick. You know, in China, White Deer are good luck. Bái lù. They're supposed to bring long life or something."

Drew typed 'White Deer New York' into his phone and found an article titled 'Seneca White Deer'. "Oh, this is cool. There's a rare herd of White Deer living in an old army depot in Seneca County. They've got this recessive gene thing called leucism, which makes them white. That must be where it came from."

"Seneca? That's like three hundred miles away," said Ryan.

"Well, must have got lost."

"Huh… anyhoo," said Ryan, returning to his phone.

He watched Ryan lying on the couch, mouth half-open and tongue looped over. He often wore this vacant expression when distracting himself on his phone, which was most of the time. Ryan didn't like sitting in his feelings. He thought being chill made him strong, but Drew knew otherwise; that the messy, uncomfortable stuff he avoided was there to keep him out of danger. Right now, he was oblivious to the storm heading his way, playing FarmVille or something equally numbing. "What you doing?"

"Trading," he said.

"Going well?"

"Always," he winked, running a hand through his sleek black curls. Ryan was handsome, with tan skin and high cheekbones. Drew had always been jealous of his hairless body, hating the spider legs sprouting from his chest and past his navel. He'd tried to have them waxed, but the pain was mind-blowing, and they grew back within a month. Ryan looked effortless and moisturised, even after a night of partying, while Drew still got pimple breakouts whenever he shaved.

"I'm finding it stressful these days… trading. Trying to time the top…"

Ryan blew a raspberry. "Man… you think too much. Gotta be zen about it. It's just math. Math is chill."

When Ryan lost control of his chill, it usually took the form of rage. All the pressure from keeping his feelings in check burst out, raining hot bile. Charlotte caught the worst of it but gave as good as she got. When they argued, it went on for days.

"Where's Grey? Still asleep?"

Ryan scratched his balls. "Dunno. We were up pretty late last night. Probably still sleeping."

"Sleeping? I didn't know he did that."

Ryan wasn't listening. Whatever he was looking at on his phone had him hooked. Drew felt the weight of Charlotte's confession on his shoulders. He didn't like lying to his friend and already dreaded taking sides. "I'm going to check on Grey… see if he's still alive," said Drew, looking for an excuse to leave.

"Give him a high-five from me," said Ryan.

"For what?"

"For being the fastest coder in the frickin' US," he said, flipping onto his belly and kicking his legs.

On the landing, Drew heard the sound of the bathtub being filled. He knocked on the door and called out to see if Charlotte was okay. She opened the door a crack, and pillowy steam rolled out. "You good?"

"Yeah, I'm all good."

"Great. Oh… apparently, there's a herd of White Deer out by Seneca. That must have been where it came from."

"Oh… cool," was all she said.

"I'm gonna wake Grey up: start thinking about lunch."

She nodded. Drew hovered for a few more seconds, trying to work out if she was being deliberately frosty or drained from the last twenty-four hours. "Okay, well, shout if you need anything."

"Thanks," she blinked at him before closing the door.

What a mess, he thought. What this house needed was Grey's neutrality, somebody who he could chat shit with guilt-free. He'd even talk about work if it came to it, anything to forget the cloud hanging over them.

He knocked on Grey's door. "You up?" When no answer came, he let himself in. The room was empty, and the bed was made as if nobody had slept in it. Grey wasn't the type to smooth the sheets or plump the pillows before his day began. His laptop and red headphones were on the bedside table, but there was no sign of the hands and head they were usually attached to. He walked to the en-suite. "Hey bro, you in there?" The door creaked open. It was also empty, and nothing seemed unusual except for an earthy smell that hung in the air.

"That's odd... Grey!" He shouted into the hallway. Grey wasn't the type to go for walks, either. "Rye... is Grey down..." The words stuck in his throat. He was looking at one of the landscape paintings in Grey's bedroom: sheep grazing in a green field. Something was wrong, though. On one of the small hills stood a lone figure, tall and dressed in black. He squinted at it and then back at the bedside table. "Are you fuckin'..." The tall figure watching the flock was wearing red headphones. He reached out and touched the painting, and when he drew his hand away, a gooey paint trail followed. It was fresh. Adrenaline frosted his veins. "RYAN! RYE! You gotta come see this!"

He heard Ryan grumble from the living room, followed by shuffling footsteps.

"So many stairs..." he groaned. "What's happened?"

Drew pointed at the painting. "Tell me that isn't a pair of

red headphones."

"What are you..." and then he saw it. His face crinkled. "Is that...?"

"Grey? Looks like it. And look..." Drew pressed his thumb into the figure's head, leaving it smeared. "Can't be more than a couple of hours old."

Ryan looked at Drew and raised an eyebrow. "Ha ha, very funny."

"No, man, I'm not messing with you. I was looking for Grey, and... I can't find him."

Ryan turned around into the hallway and shouted, "GREY! Get your ass up here!"

Drew grabbed his arm. "I'm telling you, he's gone."

"Gone? Gone where? You couldn't pay that guy to get fresh air."

"GREY!" They both shouted together.

"Where's Charlotte?" Said Ryan, looking nervous.

"In the bathroom..."

Ryan stamped away, and Drew followed, his heart stamping, too. Ryan was a serial prankster, but this was too high-brow for his style, and Grey didn't have a sense of humour, which meant that only Charlotte could be responsible.

"Hey! Charlotte!" called Ryan, banging on the door. "Did you..."

The door opened before he got the words out, and Grey stepped out, his cheeks flushed.

"Dude... what the fuck?" Ryan pushed the door open and saw Charlotte lying in the tub under a cloud of bubbles.

Drew gaped at Grey, his mind spiralling. There was no reasonable explanation for any of this. "Grey. What's going on?"

"Nothing," he said sheepishly, his eyes fixed on the floor.

"Nothing?" said Ryan, shoving Grey in the shoulder. "You're chilling with my naked girlfriend..."

"Hey!" snapped Charlotte, her voice echoing around the

tiles. "We were just talking."

He turned to her, eyes blazing. "What was so important that it couldn't wait until you were wearing clothes?"

"Oh, come on... you're being gross."

"Are you fucking serious?!"

Drew got between Ryan and Charlotte and tried to calm him down. He sympathised, and part of him felt jealous, too. If she had just confided in Grey, whatever bond they had made in the creek wasn't special anymore; it felt like he was Grey's warm-up act, which was crazy because Grey was the last person anyone should turn to for relationship advice. He'd never even been on a date. "Look... It's all good. We found Grey, but... what about the painting?"

"What about it?" said Charlotte.

Drew turned to her, but he couldn't meet her eye.

"Someone... has painted Grey into one of Frost's landscapes."

"What?" said Grey.

"Someone? It was clearly Charlotte," said Ryan, spinning away in frustration.

"Um... I have no idea what you are talking about. I've been out all morning with Drew."

Drew nodded. That was true, but now Ryan was looking at him with suspicion. "Well, clearly, it was one of you."

Charlotte began to stand up, hands covering her stomach. Ryan's mouth fell open, and Grey looked away. "Drew, hand me a towel."

Ryan pushed past Drew and threw it at her. She shook her head at him. "Fucking men."

"Okay. So nobody is going to own up to doing the painting?" said Drew, trying to divert Ryan away from the bait. Everybody stayed silent. "So... it was already there before we got here. That's the only explanation. A random coincidence. It's not Grey."

Charlotte wrapped the red towel around her and walked out of the bathroom, water dripping from her legs. "Show me."

Charlotte examined the painting closely, wiggling her finger in the black paint. Grey peered over her shoulder with a look of complete confusion. "Hey... those are my headphones."

"Yeah. This was done recently," agreed Charlotte. She pulled her finger away and stuck it in her mouth.

"Jesus, Charlotte, what the fuck?" said Ryan.

"Relax... It's just what I thought. Dirt," she said, spitting it out. "Dirt mixed with something else... it's bitter."

"Dirt? Like from the ground?" Ryan looked horrified.

"No, like from the sky." She spat again, this time near his bare feet.

Ryan was about to retaliate when Drew snatched the painting off the wall and began marching it downstairs.

"Drew?" Their three faces appeared over the bannisters.

Drew didn't consciously know why he had decided to take the painting, only that his guts were squirming, and he wanted it out of the house. He walked onto the porch and set it down against a tree, facing away from the lodge. "It's not right," he said as Ryan and Charlotte reached the door. "I know it seems like I'm overreacting, but that's... too weird."

"What? Like cursed?" Said Ryan, a smile creeping back into his mouth.

"Well... unless one of us is playing the long game with this prank, then... I don't know what to tell you. Someone must have snuck into the house and done it while we were out this morning."

"Like who?" scoffed Ryan.

Drew stared at Charlotte. Ryan laughed. "Oh, come on, you fucking wimps. There's literally zero, zero, zero chance that Robert Frost did this. Not a chance in hell. Do you think he's out there hiding in the woods? Are you serious?"

Drew remembered how Charlotte looked at the creek: Pulsing eyes and bloodless skin. He was almost certain she'd seen one of Seneca's White Deer, but now doubt was worming in through the cracks. "I mean, no... of course not. Right?" Drew looked at Charlotte.

"Yeah... absolutely not."

"Right!" laughed Ryan. "So, let's not get paranoid. Nothing's wrong. We're all here, safe and sound."

Drew nodded but hated that he couldn't explain what had happened. "So... should I bring it back in?" Drew pointed to the painting. "I don't want to freak out over nothing. I'm not, am I? It is... strange."

"Maybe leave it under the porch, just in case it rains," volunteered Charlotte. "Back on the property."

Drew picked it up but kept it facing away from him. "Good plan. But seriously, what..."

Grey's body hit the roof of the porch with a wet slap.

Drew dropped the painting and stumbled backwards. Ryan and Charlotte, standing under the porch's roof, ran outside to see what had happened. Charlotte's scream tore through the forest. Ryan's hands shot to his head, and he almost tripped over Drew, shaking amongst the yellow leaves.

The impact had virtually decapitated Grey. His long neck was folded in half, and a shard of bone split the skin where it had snapped. Above, white curtains drifted from an open window. Charlotte's scream had frightened away all the sounds of the woods, and the three stood in frozen silence.

Grey breathed.

"Oh my god... Grey..." cried Charlotte, falling forward.

He burbled, and blood cascaded from his mouth and down his cheek. His leg twitched, and then he was gone.

5

T he first thought that clawed its way to the surface was that he had jumped, and that made Drew vomit all over Ryan's bare legs. Charlotte was kneeling, her hands clasped, praying to the monster that used to be Grey, who lay coiled on the porch roof.

The first person to act was Ryan. He hoisted himself up the wooden cross beams and onto the platform. When he touched Grey, he winced as if he had just grabbed a hot stove, and tears jumped from his eyes.

"What do I do?" He wailed.

Drew's entire head felt like it had pins and needles. He stumbled towards the porch, his legs numb and wobbling. "We need to get him down." His voice had never sounded so small.

"No, don't move him," cried Charlotte.

"We have to," said Drew, pushing away her cloying hands.

"FUCK!" Screamed Ryan. "FUCK, FUCK, FUCK!"

Drew's soul had left his body when he threw up. He didn't cry or shout; he just held up his arms, beckoning

Ryan to lower their friend down.

"I can't, man... Grey's... he's fuckin' six-five."

Drew lowered his arms and looked back at Charlotte. "What did you say to him in there?"

"What?" Her face was swollen and red.

"In the bathroom." Drew walked over to her and grabbed her shoulder.

"Hey!" Ryan thudded to the floor, tearing Drew's arm away.

"Grey wouldn't do this. This isn't him. You said something." Drew's voice was monotone, and he swayed with the wind.

Charlotte slapped him across the face. Feeling returned to him for a split second, but the void was stronger. His lids drooped. "You're lying to me. What did you do? What did you tell him?"

She was about to strike him again, but Ryan caught her arm. "Stop it! Both of you... fuck. Not now."

Drew turned to Ryan. "Grey wasn't like that. Not now. Not ever." His words were soft and deliberate.

They all knew he was right. Grey's life was a monoculture; he was happy doing the same thing every day; it was his dream. That's what they had believed anyway.

Drew was floating, watching the face-off from above while his childhood friend's blood pattered between them. "She's not told you everything... She's lying to you too..."

Ryan pushed him, and he toppled to the ground. His head hit the floor, and a million stars exploded. As he lay there, stunned, reality drained back in, and it felt like venom. Drew began to cry. "Oh... shit... oh, no, no."

Ryan crouched, facing into the gloomy forest, saying nothing.

"Guys... guys... we've got to call an ambulance." Charlotte glanced up at Grey's body and then away very quickly. "We should call the police too."

"Why?" said Ryan.

"Drew's right… There's no way he jumped. I didn't say anything to him. Honestly…" She tried to touch Ryan, but he pushed her away. "Nothing that would make him do anything like that." She turned to Drew now. "Please, believe me."

"So what are you saying? Huh? That someone pushed him out the window?" yelled Ryan. "We were all up there just now; no one else is in the house…" His face distorted. "Jesus CHRIST!"

Drew sat up, Grey's body bending in and out of focus. "Who's got a phone? Mine's inside."

Ryan threw his iPhone at him, and it bounced off his arm. It showed no signal. "I need to get closer to Grey's… router. There's no service out here."

"No!" said Charlotte.

Drew knew what she was thinking: There was someone else inside, and that someone had killed Grey. "I've got to."

"Then I'll come with you…" said Charlotte.

"Ryan, we're heading in."

He didn't reply; he just stared into the woods.

A hushed calm had filled the lodge since they left. Even though the curtains in Grey's bedroom flapped in the breeze, a thick smell of dust, cobwebs, and dirt filled their nostrils. It didn't make sense.

"Are you okay?" Said Charlotte. The look on her face told him she knew it was a stupid question, but that's not why she asked it. She needed him to be present with her now. "I really didn't…"

He stopped her on the landing, both of them framed by a painting of a winter landscape covered in snow. "You were about to tell me something down at the creek? What was it? Did you tell Grey? Are you fucking him? What it is it?" He knew he sounded crazy for asking, but he needed to make sense of the doubt gnawing at his insides.

"What?" Charlotte looked like she was about to be sick.

"Oh my god... who? Grey?!" She backed away. "How could you say that?" She began to cry.

"I'll love you no matter what you say. And I'll never tell a soul, Rye, or anyone, but I need to know... because there's no other explanation. You said something to him in there that made him... that made him..." Drew shook silently, tears streaming.

"Is that what you think of me?"

"THEN WHAT THE FUCK HAPPENED!"

She flinched, clutching her stomach. "I told him... that I was leaving." Her voice was ragged.

"What? Leaving where? Here? The lodge?"

Charlotte sank to her knees, her face scrunched in pain, clutching her abdomen. "No... leaving the company. Totem. I can't stay, not after everything with Ryan, I wanted him to be the first to know... He built it. He made it all real. Without him, it was just an idea... meaningless. Oh my god... he's dead."

Drew collapsed to his knees, shame, self-loathing and anger all whirling inside him. He knocked his head against the bannister. "I'm a fucking freak. I'm... I'm sorry... I just... this can't be happening!"

She held him, and he held her, and together, they rocked and cried until it hurt, and their eyes felt raw. Drew cradled her head, feeling his heart beating against her cheek. Their friend was lying less than ten feet away. He was here half an hour ago, and now, he would never be again.

"Are you okay?" Drew wiped his face and nodded to her hands, which were still clawing into her ribs.

"It's nothing..." she sniffed, pulling them away self-consciously. "Come on, we've got to call the police."

He lifted her up and helped her through the door, shielding each other from the window. The router was on the bedside table, but the lights, which normally flashed green, were dull. Drew picked it up and turned it around. "What..." he spun it around again. "No, no, no, no..."

"What's wrong?"

Drew held up the router. The power cord had been severed, with frayed red and copper wires twisting from its casing.

"Wait... who would... surely Grey would never..." said Charlotte.

"No. There's no way... there's only one explanation. The painting... Grey... now this..." He turned to her. "Someone else is in the house."

Charlotte charged down the stairs and out the door, throwing herself into Ryan's arms. He held her close, glaring at Drew, who was hot on her heels. "You called them? Are they coming?"

Drew felt Grey's absence hanging above him. A nightmare was on the roof, and if he let it, it would suck away all the resolve he needed to deal with whatever was coming. Grief was the temptress on his right shoulder, fear the demon on his left. "We've got a problem."

"Oh god!" Cried Ryan, his eyes drawn to Grey's twisted body. "What?"

"The router's been... sabotaged."

"What do you mean?"

"Someone's slashed the cable. It's dead."

Ryan looked like he was juggling chainsaws in his mind, a hundred emotions buzzing on his face. "What are you saying? Are you saying Grey did this? Why would he do this?" He was about to explode.

"Baby..." said Charlotte, stroking his face. "I don't think he would. Someone is here in the house with us. I think... someone killed Grey."

Then, Ryan's eyes went cold. He pushed Charlotte away and walked into the house. Standing in the middle of the foyer, he tipped his head back and looked up at the three floors. "Hey!" Two tears fled down his cheeks. "HEY! I'm going to give you a minute to come out, you piece of shit. And then, I'm gonna fucking come up there and rip your throat out through your mouth."

Charlotte began to sob. Drew stood there watching Ryan swell with rage.

"I'm gonna mash you into fucking pulp. OKAY?"

The house was quiet.

"The police are coming, and you better pray they get here before I find you." He started walking up the stairs. "Think you can kill my friend and get away with it?" His face burst, but he recovered. Drew followed behind. If someone were in the house, he'd have to back Ryan to the death. They stalked through the floors. The smell of damp earth was everywhere. Ryan picked up an ornamental poker from one of the fireplaces and, holding it like a sword, checked each bedroom, closet and bathroom. Nothing seemed out of place. "This is fucked," he said once they had cleared the entire house.

"What are we going to do?" Said Drew.

"The only thing we can. Take the SUV and drive to the nearest town. It's only twenty minutes away."

"Do we leave... him here?" Drew felt utterly drained.

"I don't know."

"I don't want to leave him," said Drew.

"Well, one of us could go, and two could stay."

"I can't drive." Drew was a city boy through and through. He'd never needed to learn, but now he wished he had. He wanted to get away.

Ryan rubbed his face. "Right. Okay, I'll go then."

"I don't think we should waste any time."

Ryan looked like he was about to say something but thought better of it. Then, the horror of what had happened bled back in, and his face fell. "Yeah... you two going to be okay?"

"I think we should stay outside."

They couldn't see Grey's body from where they were standing, which was worse in some ways—the absence.

"Oh my god... Totem..." said Ryan.

"Yeah, look, we can't think about that now."

"He kept the whole thing going." Ryan looked haunted. "Fuck…"

"We prepared for something like this… well, not this… but we all have full access to the repo. It'll just be a case of…" Drew suddenly remembered that he had decided to leave, as had Charlotte. He felt okay about resigning when Grey was still there to man the helm, but now Totem would be Ryan alone, which seemed an impossible challenge. "Let's just forget about it for now."

"Man, we've got plates spinning. Investors…"

"Yeah, well, our lead dev, our friend, is dead. They'll have to suck it up."

Ryan and Grey had always been the engine behind Totem, with Charlotte and Drew providing the imagination. If it went under, they'd leave with their creativity intact, but Drew always felt Ryan would be lost without it.

"And it was all going so well. Just last night…"

Drew stopped him with a hug. He wanted to squeeze all the pain and worry out of him. Everything would be different now; there was no point in pretending otherwise, but they still had each other. Ryan was stiff at first, but then he softened and began to cry. He buried his face in the crook of Drew's neck. "Why is this happening?"

"I don't know," wept Drew. "But we're gonna make it through, okay? I've been here before with mum and dad. I just didn't think I'd be back so soon."

"I don't know how…"

"No one does."

Drew hugged him tighter.

"You should get going." He could tell Ryan didn't want to let go. "It'll be dark in a few hours."

Ryan nodded, wiping a patch of drool from Drew's shoulder. "I'll get the keys."

Charlotte was sitting on the porch. When she heard

them coming, she looked relieved. "Nothing?"

"Nothing. I will head to Tyler Hill, find a phone, and get help. You two stay here."

Charlotte didn't like that plan. "Look, we're not splitting up. Something killed Grey..."

"We don't know that," said Drew.

"Why can't we all go?" Charlotte clung to them both.

"And leave him here?" Said Drew, pointing to the dark space above their heads. "We can't leave him alone; it's not right."

She looked like she wanted to remind him that Grey was dead and dead people don't get lonely, but better sense held her tongue. She was frightened. They all were. "Why don't we at least try and lift him down? Roll him up in a sheet or something. That way, we can all get out of here. Together. The four of us," she said.

Ryan looked at Drew. It was worth a try, they agreed.

Upstairs, they took turns breaking down in tears while the others solemnly stripped the bed.

"We can lower him down, but someone needs to be at the bottom to take the strain."

"I'll... I'll do it..." sniffed Charlotte.

"You ready?" Ryan looked at Drew. Drew didn't nod.

The wind had died down, the lace curtains hanging still, and the earthy smell had grown faint.

"Let's do it," said Drew.

Ryan went out first, dropping onto the roof with a whump.

"I'll head down," said Charlotte.

"Take that." Drew pointed to the gold poker. Charlotte picked it up and looked at it in horror, as if she were playing out a scenario in her mind where she'd have to use it.

"If you see anything... scream for us," said Drew.

Ryan screamed. Charlotte snapped her head back towards the window. "Rye!"

Drew was already making his way through the window.

46

He saw Ryan pacing around the empty roof. Grey was gone, and all that was left was a dark stain.

"No, no, no, no…"

Charlotte screamed, too, making them both jump.

"Okay. Okay. What the… WHAT THE FUCK!" Ryan punched the wooden cladding, and his hand popped. He sank to the ground, holding his twisted knuckles.

"He's not on the ground either," said Drew. "I can't see him!" His thoughts moved in slow motion. If they hadn't seen somebody moving the body in the handful of minutes they had been inside, they would have heard it. Grey was long with big bones; moving him would be a noisy struggle. "Fuck this… let's get out of here," he said.

Ryan let out a gasp. "I think I've broken my hand."

"Charlotte, you'll have to drive," Drew said.

As he looked up at her, he saw a pair of hands gripping the window frame on either side of her shoulders. The curtains danced. "Charlotte…"

She saw the way Drew looked at her, and her eyelids fluttered. Two rows of yellow teeth and a shrivelled chin rested on her head. Drew reached up and grabbed her shirt, yanking her out the window. She fell on top of him and knocked the wind out of his stomach.

Ryan jumped up. "What the fuck, man!"

Drew was struggling to breathe, but the noises he was making, honking and rasping as he watched the sunken eyes fade into the gloom of Grey's bedroom, were as much from fear as pain. "I… I…"

Charlotte was touching her head. She knew she'd felt something but had no idea what it was. "I'm fine," said Charlotte, standing up. "Let's just… get to the car."

"Guys, wait… up…" Drew wretched. "The window…"

The roof gave way with a groan and a crack. Ryan fell through first, his trailing hand wildly grabbing Charlotte's ankle. Drew tried to crunch forward, but gravity sucked him after them, and they landed in a heap of dust and splintered wood on the porch steps.

Ryan coughed and rolled onto the drive, a cloud of grey dust pluming off him. "Charlotte... what the..."

Charlotte shot upwards, eyes wide, completely dazed. "I'm okay, I'm okay... I think." She turned to Drew, who was lying on his back, wheezing from the second impact.

"That's it. I'm bringing the car around. Help him up." Ryan scrambled to his feet, stumbled a few steps and then face-planted into a pile of leaves. He swore and crawled towards where his SUV had been parked.

Charlotte began heaving a plank of wood away from Drew's arm. He had a deep, pink cut across his forehead. "It's not too bad. You're gonna be fine," she said.

He grabbed her arm. "There was... something... behind you..."

"What? Where?"

"Yellow hands..."

They heard Ryan's voice screaming from the forest. "No! No! You fuckin'! Shit! Fuckin'! No!"

Ryan was limping as fast as he could into the woods. Charlotte sprinted after him, leaving Drew lying in the nest of roof parts. His eyes followed them through the trees. At first, he couldn't make sense of it. It looked like the car had been cut in half, its back wheels raised into the air. Then he heard splashing as Ryan entered the water and realised that the SUV had somehow rolled down through the clearing and into the lake.

He knew for sure now: none of this was a coincidence and they weren't alone.

6

"So, who's going to be the first person to say it?" Ryan was sitting on the couch, wrapped in towels while Charlotte cleaned Drew's wound with cotton wool, which was dark orange with blood.

Grey was dead, worse, dead and gone. The SUV was unsalvageable, they had no reception, and nobody expected them back in New York for another six days. None of them had the strength to confront the truth of their situation, but someone had to.

"So... you saw something," said Ryan.

"I saw hands and a face... well, part of a face. Standing up there in Grey's bedroom behind Charlotte." Drew looked up at her. "I know you felt it."

Her eyes flitted nervously towards Ryan, but she didn't confirm or deny it.

"Who was it? A man? I know you want to say it... so say it." Ryan looked pissed.

Drew sat up, facing him. "Is it so weird? After everything that's happened? We're staying in the house of a guy who vanished into the creek without a trace. Never confirmed dead. In fact, from what I've read, no one knows anything."

"Yeah, that happened like thirty years ago! Get a grip. He'd be like… seventy by now. We're talking about a person who can shift bodies and move in silence. Does that sound plausible to you?"

None of it did, but Drew knew when Ryan was keeping something from him. He had an easy tell; he got defensive. "So what do you think happened?"

Ryan threw his hands up in the air. "I don't know…"

Drew looked at Charlotte, who was fidgeting by the mantlepiece. Unlike Ryan, Charlotte didn't get angry when she was hiding something; she got sad.

"What about you? You think I'm crazy?"

Charlotte bit her lip.

"Look, one of you is gonna tell me what's going on… because I'm not blind, I can see something's eating at you… and it's not just what happened to Grey."

He stood up, and a dull ache sunk through his head. "Whatever it is, I don't care. There's an explanation… for everything. But we need to be honest with each other to start working out how we get out of this. So… if you know anything or have any inkling or theory about what's happening here, speak now. Because… I'm fucking terrified and confused."

It was only a subtle gesture, a parting of the lips, fingers curling into a fist, the glint of a tear. Charlotte wanted to say something. Ryan shut it down. "No, Charlotte, we're not going there."

Drew slammed the flat of his hand down on the coffee table. "Grey is dead! You could tell me you fucking killed him for all I care, but at least I'd know. Do I need to say it?" His mouth was dry, and his head was pounding. "We're sitting ducks here! Is that what you want? Charlotte… pushed out the window. Me?"

Ryan clenched his jaw.

"We need to tell him," said Charlotte.

"Grey is not dead because..." yelled Ryan, "Because of us."

Drew sat down beside Ryan and stared at him. "Just fucking tell me, man... let me decide for myself. Look, I already had to deal with all that secrecy at the beginning of the trip. I know you were doing it for fun, but it's not fun anymore. So please..."

Ryan sighed, and it felt like the room got a little darker. "The cousin... the one we hired the place off..."

"For $90 a night, which is fucking insane," said Drew.

"You gonna let me finish?"

Charlotte stepped forward, but Ryan stopped her with a raised finger. "She told us that... under no circumstances were we to touch any of Robert Frost's paintings."

"Touch? Like touch with our hands? What does that mean?" Drew felt blood souring his windpipe.

"We weren't to move, damage them, photograph them..."

Charlotte turned away, stuffing a sob back down her throat.

"Basically, she said that her cousin, Frost, was very protective of his paintings. She wanted his final words to be respected... she sounded a bit superstitious, to be honest..."

"Final words?"

Charlotte sighed loudly. "He didn't want them to be sold or copied... or messed with in any way. It was against his... morals. The paintings were sacred to him. Something like that."

This chimed with the interview Drew had read in *Splash.* "Okay... so what is the vibe I'm getting here? What's got you on edge?" he said.

"Well..." Ryan shot Charlotte a nervous look. "She was crazy, right? Like, paranoid about not touching the art... I don't know... I mean... the painting with the sheep and Grey in it. You..."

Drew's heart juddered. "Wait... are you talking about

me moving that painting outside? Does she have sensors in here? Cameras? Is she gonna know? Are we gonna lose our deposit? What?" His voice cracked in a nervous laugh.

Ryan's knee started to jiggle. "No man... look... the cousin... she said, that about fifteen years ago..."

"In 2010," confirmed Charlotte.

"Right. Okay... there's no easy way to say this... but a couple stayed here, two artists, on a kinda retreat. Apparently, they were getting creative with some of the artwork in the house... taking them into the woods, doing weird video shoots... like, interpretive dance shit, stuff that nobody watches anyway."

Drew could see his hands were shaking, and it wasn't from the cold.

"Basically, they were found drowned in the lake out there. And... one of the paintings was floating in there too..."

Drew sat back. "Which one?"

Ryan looked out of the door into the foyer. "I don't know, man... she didn't say."

"Why didn't you say anything? You don't think it's important to let me know two people died staying here? We're in the fucking wilderness!"

"Because... it's a vibe kill."

"A vibe kill?"

"We wanted it to be fun! We did this for you!" Ryan looked at Charlotte, imploring her to back him up.

"We did, Drew... honestly," she said, but it wasn't convincing.

Drew wanted to believe they'd been thinking of him, that Charlotte had remembered those gentle mornings spent with him, watching Robert Frost paint fern trees with hair combs and honey. But he knew there was more to this. "I'm confused. Are you saying that because I moved that painting out of the house, we're what... marked? That I'm gonna end up in the fucking lake?"

Ryan laughed, but it sounded like a fly shaken in a bottle, a weak buzz. "No, man…"

"I would have never touched anything if you'd told me this before."

Charlotte knelt at their feet and gazed up at Drew, trying to reassure him. "We didn't believe the cousin… some crazy old lady… Robert Frost isn't doing this to us. This isn't some beyond-the-grave vendetta."

"But you do believe her now?" he said. Their silence was a swamp. Drew staggered up before it sucked him down and walked to the door. "I'm not fucking staying here. Nope."

"Where you gonna go?" Said Charlotte.

"I'm gonna walk to the nearest town. We all are."

"Drew… it's miles away. And it's dark out."

Drew felt panic, and his circuits began to fry. No matter how deeply he breathed, he couldn't catch any air, and his heart squelched in his ears. "Are you really considering staying? Our best friend is dead! I know what I saw behind you up there. I'm telling you… something is after us…" He stared at them wild-eyed. "There's a reason Grey was painted in that picture. It was a warning. An omen…" The last word stuck in his throat like a brick. "Oh my god. Have we checked the other paintings in the house?"

"For what?" Said Ryan.

"For… us."

As he dashed through the lodge, Charlotte and Ryan followed cautiously, Drew felt like he was running through his own mind, trying to determine what was real and what wasn't. The revelation that two people had died at the lodge in connection with one of the paintings was sickening. Every door he pushed open, he expected to see himself painted into the rolling hills or lying face down in a stream. Room after room, he searched until he was down to the last: his own.

"Nothing?" Said Charlotte.

Drew didn't say anything; he just stood staring at his

closed door.

"Are you going in?" Ryan stood behind Charlotte.

Drew took a deep breath and entered, disappearing into the dark. They didn't follow. Drew returned a moment later, shaking his head. "Nothing."

They both looked relieved. Ryan let out a bitter laugh. "Okay. So, where does this leave us?"

Drew didn't want to be the one with the answers, but his gut was screaming at him to run. "I say we go."

"I don't... I don't know if we should," said Charlotte.

"You think it's more dangerous out there than in here?"

"I mean..."

Drew took Charlotte's hands. "Look, I think you saw something down in the creek. I saw it, too, but it wasn't hiding behind a rock; it was standing right behind you..." he pointed to Grey's room.

"No, that was a deer. We saw it." Charlotte fumbled with her phone and brought up the photo she had taken of the Seneca White Deer. She showed it to Ryan. "See?"

He peered at it and then leapt back as if electrocuted. "Are you fucking with me?!"

Drew grabbed the phone. He saw the deer with its bony behind angled high into its right hip as it sloped away through the trees. "What?"

"The fucking tree man. The fucking tree!"

They crowded around the screen while Ryan jabbed his finger at the trunk of a thick pine. Charlotte let out a cry. A grimy, bearded face, half obscured by the tree, peered out with hollow eyes. "Oh my god," whispered Drew. "It... he... was following us. Is that... Robert Frost?" It was impossible to tell. Whoever it was, they looked like a ghost or an ancient ancestor of the human species.

"I'm not going out there, man," said Ryan, his voice the texture of running water. "Someone... something's out there."

Drew turned to Charlotte. He needed her to back him up.

"I don't know what's going on here. But… if we don't leave, we're asking to be picked off one by one."

"This isn't happening!" yelled Ryan. "I knew we should have gone to fuckin' Miami!"

Drew could tell Charlotte was conflicted, but he still felt like there was something she wasn't telling him. "I'm not saying that's Robert Frost…" he said, pointing at the screen, "But I think he… it… is a killer. We need help."

She nodded and then shook her head in quick succession.

"Please, tell me, what's so confusing about this situation? You guys booked the fucking place and left me in the dark. Well… I've got the final say now. We're going."

"You're the one who moved the picture, man…" said Ryan.

Drew's body seized up, and his fists clenched. "So what? You're saying this is my fucking fault? I had no idea…"

"No!" Charlotte got between them. "No one is saying that. We're all scared. I think… Drew's right. We should go."

Drew looked defiantly at Ryan. It was two against one. "Okay. Get your things and meet downstairs in five minutes. Only the essentials."

"Fine," muttered Ryan, "But if we get…"

"No one is getting blamed for anything," snapped Charlotte. "We're all in this together."

Ryan threw his hands up. "Right."

Drew returned to his room and stuffed his clothes and electronics in a rucksack. He'd never thought about needing a weapon before, but he'd head down to the kitchen and pick out the longest, sharpest knife he could find. Drew didn't believe in ghosts, demons or monsters. He believed that, despite the inhumanity he'd witnessed in the last few hours, whatever had killed Grey was mortal, and it would bleed if he stuck it.

He picked up his phone and started closing tabs to conserve battery. Only 42 per cent remained. When he came to the *Splash* interview with Robert Frost, his thumb hovered over it. He wondered if Frost really could be hiding in the woods, terrorising anyone who messed with his paintings. His radical beliefs were clear, but surely they were not strong enough to empower him with superhuman abilities and a desire for murderous revenge.

It would all have been so much simpler if it weren't for the painting Ryan had revealed on their first night. There was something messianic and unhinged about it that set Drew's heart on a tilt. He'd wanted to know the truth before, but now he just wanted to run.

Drew ignored the landscape painting of the lake beside his door on his way out. He hadn't wanted to tell Charlotte and Ryan about the freshly painted naked torso he'd found when he'd checked a few minutes earlier: a man staring at his reflection with slicked black hair. Its discovery wouldn't help them, and he needed to keep them sane.

He headed down the stairs, Ryan and Charlotte bickering above. Drew ransacked the drawers, finding a blunt carving knife that was heavy-duty enough to do damage if he put his back into it. He slipped it into the inside pocket of his Calvin Klein jacket and left, leaving all the drawers open.

He waited by the entrance, the dining room door open enough to see the cloaked painting lurking in the corner. "You guys ready?" He shouted.

"Almost!"

He clenched his jaw. The garish paintings hanging around the brown foyer turned his stomach. He couldn't wait to see the back of this place. "Hurry up!"

Drew didn't want to think about leaving Grey here, alone and cold, and already dreaded the fresh nightmares of him shaking and rattling in the ground as steam billowed from his open jaws, the same nightmares that haunted him after his parents passed. His life was slowly turning into a graveyard.

"Ready!" shouted Charlotte as Ryan leapt the last three steps.

"Thank fuck. Let's get out of here."

"Don't forget me," came a voice from the dining room.

Their collective inhalation could have sucked up the lake. It was Grey's voice—no doubt about it.

"He's alive!" whispered Charlotte hoarsely, making for the door.

"No..." Drew grabbed her and pulled them back into the house. "There's no way... his neck. He was gone."

"Then... who was..."

The sound of footsteps scuttling made them all yell out. Drew ran to slam the dining room door just in time to see a tall, hunched figure shrouding itself under the painting's black cloak.

"Run!"

And they did, into the woods.

7

Frantic breathing and the sound of cracking branches accompanied their escape. Ryan was out in front, ripping through the trees while Drew kept pace with Charlotte. Darkness swallowed the path behind them, its teeth champing at their heels.

"Guys..."

The air was biting cold, stunning Drew's lungs. If they didn't pause for rest soon, he thought he'd pass out, but adrenaline was his captain now, and it felt like his legs might carry him even after he lost consciousness. When they reached a small clearing, he called out to the other. "Guys... wait... we don't know where we're going."

Ryan wheeled around, eyes wide. "Fuck!"

Charlotte leant against a tree, panting. "We need to head north. Get the compass out on your phone. It'll work without reception."

"Mine's almost dead, you..." Ryan stopped in front of Charlotte. "Babe... why the fuck are you carrying that painting."

Charlotte looked down. She was indeed holding the

painting of Grey with his smudged head.

Drew ran his hands through his hair, "Charlotte... no..."

"I heard his voice. You both did, too!"

Ryan grabbed the painting and hurled it into the dark.

"After everything we've talked about, why would you do that?" said Drew, not angry but defeated.

"This is all we have left of him."

"You don't think..."

"It's just a fucking painting!" She shrieked, standing up and going after it.

Drew ran after her and pulled her back to face him. "I know, I know. It doesn't make sense, but something is seriously wrong with that house and everything in it."

Ryan barreled past them and picked up the painting, lying face-up. Its white sky caught the moonlight, and he raised his fist to punch a hole in it.

"Rye... no!" Said Drew.

He paused mid-strike.

"Don't fucking Rye me! Charlotte's right; it's just a painting," he turned to the wilderness, "And to whoever is fucking with us... I'm not hiding anymore! I'm not running! Come out and get me!" He puffed up his chest and roared into the night. "There's nothing spooky going on here. Just a sicko who is about to get fucked up. I'll... I'll kill him for what he did... for what he did..." he was beginning to hyperventilate, and his knees shook.

Drew caught him before he fell and held him tight. "We need to focus on getting out of here. We're barely half a mile away and already spent."

Ryan began to laugh. "We're exhausted... terrified... I haven't eaten since last night. We'll be lost within the hour. No man... I'm not running. I need to face this thing."

Drew gave Charlotte a pleading look. If Ryan unravelled now, they'd be done for. "Rye... I mean, Ryan. We are not killers..."

Ryan had tears in his eyes. "Bro, please, let me, I'm

begging you. I can't run. I don't run."

Ryan had transformed back into the little boy Drew had known all those years ago; angry and confused, calling for his mum when he got his bike stolen by the older kids from school. He wanted to fight that day, but Drew hadn't let him. They were bigger than him, and he would have had his teeth knocked out, but he didn't care.

"No, Ryan. I won't let you."

"But that thing… man… whatever it was that you saw, killed our friend. Totem… everything, he was there for all of it. And now he's gone." He began to weep. "Our business is totally fucked… and you don't even care."

"I do care…"

"No, you don't. You never did. You always thought it was beneath you. I know how you looked at Grey and me. That's why you want to run. You never fight for anything."

Drew felt faint. This was not the time or the place. He looked for Charlotte, but she was rocking against the tree in another world.

"You've been quiet quitting for months. You're never online, you skip meetings… I give you a pass because you're my best friend, but that shit gets to me!"

"Ryan…" Drew stumbled.

"Tell me you're not leaving Totem! Tell me you weren't going to fuck off!! You could have talked to me, man."

"Now is not the time!" Drew said, squeezing him.

"This might be the last time you can come clean, bro. I thought we were ride or die…"

"I am… We are…"

Ryan grabbed Drew by the throat. "Don't leave me, man!"

Drew let Ryan grip him, his eyes welling up. He thought about all the unsaid things growing rotten inside of him, about what Charlotte had told him, and it broke his heart.

"Don't run. Not this time."

But Drew couldn't stay and fight because there was

nothing left to fight against, just a ghost from the past that had come to pick them off one by one.

"Ryan, we need to go."

"I did this for you!" He screamed into Drew's ear so loud it sounded like an explosion. "All of this… coming here was our big break!"

Drew recoiled and fell into the leaves. "Fuck… man… what… what are you talking about?"

Ryan was crying now, mighty sobs rolling out his throat. "Frost… his art… he never copyrighted any of his works… they're all public domain, which means completely fair game, and we were gonna be the first."

Drew's heart sank like a bag of puppies. Somehow, he'd known but hadn't listened to his guts yelping out.

"It had it all: the lore, the infamy, the mystery, the rarity… a fuckin' legit one-of-one collector's item." Ryan licked tears from his lips. "This was the big one. This was gonna put us on the map."

Drew's vision began to haze.

"We were gonna tell you, we were gonna do it together at the end of the trip as a big surprise, but then we got fuckin' high… I got excited… We photographed Frost's painting and uploaded it to the site. I told Grey to put it up for live auction… And it sold, man… It was huge… I'm talking all-time high… it was a feeding frenzy."

Drew stood up and walked away because he might have broken Ryan's jaw if he had stayed.

"No more shilling $200 jpegs to morons. The last time I checked, Frost's final painting had been traded for $450,000. In one night! It's probably at a million by now."

Drew stood over Charlotte. He couldn't stand to look at Ryan. "So what… this whole vacation was… a business trip? To steal Robert Frost's work?" A tear fell from his cheek and splashed on hers. "You knew about it?"

She didn't say anything.

"You let me think that it was me… that I had moved that

picture, and that's why Grey had been killed... and all the time, it was you. Even after the cousin told you not to, you knew about the couple in the lake. You lied to me."

He spun away and stood in the space between them, beneath the deep black canopy and the stars above. "You think I'm an idiot. Well..." he pointed at Charlotte while looking at Ryan. "Truth time. She's gonna fuckin' leave you, man, because you're a piece of shit. And as for you..." He turned back to Charlotte, "I've always loved you. I made my peace that you'd never see me like that, but I hoped you'd have the dignity and the respect to not use my trust in you against me."

Both of them sat in silence.

"And to cap it all off... Grey's dead. But I'm not gonna stoop to your level. I'm not gonna say he died because of you. But now I know, for all your bravado, you're too much of a coward to own the part you played." He let that hang in the air like a hawk preparing to dive. "Robert Frost was fucking right. This is what greed gets you. You take, and you take, but it'll never be enough. Are you happy now?! Fuck no."

Ryan was crying again, his face in the dirt. Charlotte looked like she'd been lobotomised. Any hope Drew had of galvanising them to escape the wilderness had been strangled. He felt cracked in two, and all the resentment was bleeding out amongst the roots, feeding the darkness around him. He knew it was over for good, but over wasn't a new job or a smaller flat anymore; it was the three of them alone in the woods, Grey dead, and something hunting them. "You fucking..." He fell to his knees and prayed that he would dissolve into the night.

Minutes passed that felt like hours until Ryan finally spoke. "You're leaving me?" He sounded small. "Why?"

Charlotte didn't respond.

"Because you're a dick," said Drew, all pretence gone.

"Well... at least you're fuckin' man enough to say it

now."

Drew chuckled. "That's rich coming from you. All these years, I didn't tell you how I felt because I thought you were too weak to take it. You act tough, but it's a facade. It's thin. You're so insecure it makes me cringe. It's pathetic."

"Oh yeah?"

Drew shook his head. "Yeah."

"So you let me walk all over you? What kind of person does that?"

Drew didn't have an answer but wanted to wound him, so he said, "Man, I've got no family left. You're my family. I put up with you because that's what family does... until they don't. And now that time's come. It's over. It's all over."

Ryan stood up. At first, Drew thought he was making his way over to hit him, but instead, he walked towards the painting lying on the ground and picked it up. "Then let's fucking finish it." He brought his fist down and through the canvas.

Drew expected it to make a tearing noise, but it crunched like a mouthful of carrots. Ryan's screech was so loud and sharp it could have severed the branches above his head. He fell to the floor and lay there writhing.

For a second, Drew considered letting him suffer, cradling the hand he'd already injured and doubtless made worse with that punch, but when the screaming didn't stop, he knew there was something wrong. Ryan's arm was squirting black all over his face. "Help me!" He screamed.

Drew couldn't fathom what he was looking at. The painting was lying beside him, a tear down the centre. Ryan's hand was sticking out through the gap, chopped halfway up the palm, oozing blood onto the canvas. Drew grabbed what was left of his wrist and tried to constrict the bleeding. "Charlotte!"

"Drew!" She responded.

He scrambled to remove his jacket and top, tying it around Ryan's stub as a makeshift tourniquet, but the blood kept on coming. "How... oh my god," he gagged. Drew cradled him from behind, Ryan sitting between his legs, and he pulled with all his might to tighten the knot. "Charlotte!"

"It fucking... bit my hand off," cried Ryan.

Charlotte ran and crouched behind them, resting her hand on Drew's shoulder.

"Where the fuck... doesn't matter, make another tourniquet." His skin had exploded with goose pimples as soon as he had taken his shirt off, and he was starting to feel numb. "Christ, it's cold. Hang in there, Rye! Charlotte... Charlotte... torniquet."

Her hand remained in place, but her grip grew tighter, squeezing the muscle above his collarbone while Drew and Ryan see-sawed in the dark, covered in black blood.

"Jesus, Charlotte, he needs you!"

She wrapped her legs around him. They felt long and hard. "Drew! Ryan!" Her voice came from a hundred yards away, up through the trees. That's when he smelled it: earth, worms, cobwebs, metal... death. Bitter fingers muffled Drew's scream. When Ryan turned around, his eyes travelled above Drew's head and kept climbing. "Drew..."

Drew convulsed as the dry fingers searched his mouth. A shadow moved across Ryan's face. Drew felt teeth on his scalp, felt them squeeze, forks of pain bursting down his neck. Ryan was petrified, holding his spade-like hand across his face as it throbbed blood. The long legs coiled around Drew's, twisting them until they creaked. Drew fought back, his hands grasping something ridged and then smooth. He hooked his fingers and pulled, eyes squeezed shut.

Then, he remembered the kitchen knife.

A rush of air. Ryan groaning. Clacking teeth as loud as stones tumbling down the creek and the sound of wet flesh being gnawed through to the bone. Drew felt a strong hand grab his shirt and yank him away to his feet and into an unsteady run. When he turned back to look for Ryan, he didn't see his head, only his body, hanging by his neck in the darkness, long yellow fingers gripping his waist.

"Don't look, don't look!" came a gravelly voice.

"Ryan!" He screamed, but Ryan was gone, dragged into the shadows with ferocious speed. Drew tried to fight, but the person pulling him away was stronger.

"Get off me... Ryan!"

"He's gone," came the disembodied voice.

Drew looked at the man hauling him through the forest and saw hollow eyes like yellow eggs set within a matted nest of grey hair. "Who... who are you?"

"Robert..." he said, as they charged towards the creek. "My name's Robert Frost."

8

Witnessing Grey's death had been enough to send Drew into the void, but Ryan's murder reminded him that he had been inside it all along. It was frightening how manipulative reality could be, wearing a mask to convince him that death wasn't staring out through its eyes. He would have begged it to take him then, but Frost whispered that Charlotte was safe, and that forced him, for better or worse, to cling on a little longer.

Frost pulled Drew through the trees, down the creek, and into a narrow cave. In its centre, a fire smouldered, and beside it lay a canvas camping bed and a bucket that smelt foul.

"Where is she?"

Frost pointed into the gloom.

"I'm here!" Charlotte looked terrified, folded up in the corner, her chin between her knees. When she saw Drew, she cried and threw her arms around him. "Where's Rye?"

Drew couldn't answer, but his silence spoke for him.

"No..." her face swallowed itself.

"I'm sorry... there was nothing I could do..." he said.

They held each other, shaking and wailing. Robert Frost stood watching them with a look of curiosity, studying their grief.

"What was that?" Said Drew.

Frost's eyes burned red in the firelight.

"What killed our friends?"

He took a seat on his camp bed and stoked the embers.

"He... he grabbed me... he..." began Charlotte before breaking down again. "I tried... to get back to you."

"I know," said Drew. "There was nothing you could have done. I'd be dead too if it weren't for..."

Robert Frost. All this time, Drew had imagined the former TV personality stalking them, but Ryan was right: Frost was just an old man. Drew recognised him beneath the matted, grey beard, but he was a shadow of his former self. The cave walls were covered in shapes and dark lines, lit one second by the fire and then snuffed out the next.

"You stole from it, didn't you?" Frost said softly.

"No..." said Drew.

"If you hadn't, then your friends would still..."

"Don't talk about my friends."

Frost nodded. Sparks cracked. "You wouldn't be the first to fall foul of it."

Drew pictured the couple floating in the golden lake, a swan pecking at their feet.

"What are you doing down here?" Said Charlotte.

"Keeping my end of a raw deal."

Drew blinked tears away. "That's not an answer. What... are you doing here? Are you hiding?"

Frost cupped his hands over the flames. "I used to be a painter... but... I never was any good at it."

"You're not getting any sympathy from me," said Drew. "Just tell us what the fuck is going on." Drew wanted to push Robert's face into the fire and watch him melt.

"No, I'm serious," and he sounded it. "I was lousy. I worked in a stockroom for fifteen years, stacking boxes. I never picked up a paintbrush in my life until..."

Charlotte moved Drew aside and took a step towards the fire.

"I used to come here as a kid. I remember seeing the lodge and thinking I'd never be able to own such a beautiful place. It was too grand for me. I hadn't earned more than $3 an hour my entire life." He scratched his beard like something was living in it. "I was up here by myself, smoking weed, being a nobody... It was the golden hour... You can feel God walking the land. The creek looked so... lovely; it felt lovelier than anything anyone had ever seen. It felt like my secret. I don't know why, probably because I was stoned out of my mind, but I decided to come back the next day and try to... um... capture it. To save it. I couldn't afford a camera, but my girlfriend... she was an actual artist, too good for me... she had supplies."

He hunched forward over the fire, his face etched with shadows, while Drew and Charlotte stood at the back of the cave, each wondering whether to run or bash his head in.

"I came a couple days every week for the next few months through winter, but I had no training and no... perspective. It was too cold to sit out most days, so I got into the habit of bringing a tent and a bottle of whisky. Well, one day in December, not a lick of paint made it on the page. I got so drunk that I ended up passing out in the snow. Not unusual for me."

He spat into the fire, and more sparks twirled in the dark. "But when I woke up... my shitty canvas was all filled up." He laughed. "You can imagine what that was like... out here in the wilderness, miles from anyone... you wake up, and BANG... someone's painted you the world, only more beautiful. I couldn't explain it. I thought I'd... uh... died or something. Gone loopy, at least."

His smile vanished. "You know... I took it home and didn't show it to anyone because... well, no one would have ever believed I'd have painted it. I was already known for telling tall tales... that's a polite way of putting it. I put it in my dad's garage and left it there for maybe two weeks. Anyway, Dad eventually found it. He liked it so much that he hung it on his wall. I never told him where it came from and he didn't ask."

Drew scanned the cave for weapons. He thought people didn't survive very long in a place like this without a gun or something deadly. He felt the carving knife weighing down his jacket pocket. He'd already been too slow to use it back in the woods, a fact he'd regret for the rest of his life, but he wouldn't miss the next opportunity.

"Now, my dad was old for his years. He forgot things. He saw things that weren't there. Well... he started saying something came out of the painting when he slept. He'd wake, and it'd be standing over him... arms raised... like this." Robert stretched his arms over his head, wrists and hands pointing in opposite directions. "I didn't believe him... but I should of. It got me thinking about what I... hadn't seen up at the creek. So, I decided to go back up there. My girlfriend had kicked me out for boozing, so I was liquor-free for a time. I could last the night without passing out. I set my canvas up, sat in my tent and waited." He shook his head. "Nothing. It rained. The paper got ruined. Waste of time... and my girlfriend's paper."

Drew kicked a pile of twigs next to the fire, scattering the embers. The wind moaned through the cave's mouth. "Where is this going?"

Frost barely reacted. "I thought that maybe it was because I was awake. I'd scared off whoever came in the night. So I returned, although this time I did something smart... an old hunting trick my dad taught me. I attached a trip wire with a bell to the easel, so if anyone moved it or walked in the vicinity, it would ring and wake me up."

Charlotte was watching him now.

"I didn't sleep well anyway, not without booze, so I took a quart with me to be safe. Enough to send me down but not knock me out." He locked eyes with her. "I remember hearing it in the pitch black. Tingle-tingle," he said as he shook his hand. "I crept out, quiet. At first, I thought it was a man. A tall man… standing there, using his fingers. I watched. I don't think I even breathed."

The cave was so dark they could barely see his face.

"It conjured it all without paint, using its nails, tongue, and prints… it was beautiful, and so… effortless. I wanted to know what it was, what it was doing… how it had found me. I waited until it had finished and was about to introduce myself when…" he chuckled wistfully, "It climbed into it."

"Climbed into it?" said Drew.

"The painting… yes. Like a thief through a window. I was, of course, shocked and… scared. It didn't make any sense. I ran my fingers over it and searched for a hole. Nothing."

"So… your dad was right."

"He was. But… I never got a chance to tell him. He died a few nights later—a heart attack. As you can imagine, I stayed away from the creek for a while… I reconnected with my girlfriend at the funeral… I sold the house. I kept the painting I'd given him and hung it on the wall in the shed at the back of my new home…. waiting for it to come out."

Charlotte and Drew had moved closer to him without realising it, drawn in by his story.

"And did it?" said Charlotte.

"Yeah…" Silence choked the cave before Robert Frost released his grip. "It came to me, and… it spoke to me."

"What was… it?"

"I don't know."

"You don't know?" Drew felt anger prickling.

"I mean… it's not real. It can't be real."

"What the fuck are you talking about? It murdered our friends… that couple in the lake. It's fuckin' real. It needs to be killed."

Robert Frost puffed out its cheeks. "The way I see it, humans are lightning rods for something greater. Sure, we take credit for it; we call it hard work, luck… it's who you know. But think about it… If Mozart had died at birth, would someone else have written 'Twinkle Twinkle Little Star'? Maybe… maybe not. We'll never know how much greatness we've missed out on… and how much evil."

"You're rambling," Drew lept forward, wanting to scare him, but Frost just sat there.

"I think it is what an artist leaves on the canvas. The thing that transports us… that takes us away to a different place in our minds, unlocks feelings, unspoken truths… poetry. Universes. It takes our fears away; it makes us forget. If I had to guess what it is, I think… it is… soul. Not a soul. Just… soul."

"It's a fucking murderer."

"Yeah. It is. But God… God's a murderer too. Capable of great inspiration and destruction. A jealous God."

Drew didn't believe any of it. It was too abstract. What he had seen was flesh and bone, with teeth and wickedness. "Let's say you're right… it is a… demon… or whatever the fuck… I think this is what you tell yourself so you don't have to face the truth… that whatever pact you made with that thing… for fame, acceptance, fortune… I don't care… has meant that people have suffered. People have died."

Robert Frost was waiting to speak before Drew had finished, his yellow teeth hanging behind thin lips. "I know people have died because of me. That doesn't mean I can explain why, or what it is, or what motivations it has for doing the things it does."

"Take a fucking guess." Drew felt the kitchen knife singing to him. "What was the deal you made?"

"I didn't know I made a deal with it until it was too late. When it crawled from the painting, its long fingers exploring the walls, thin, jointed legs, filling my shed like a Daddy Longlegs spider…. It said it wanted my help. It was worried that the world was too cynical... that the wilderness we both loved would be destroyed. It wanted to show me how to teach people to fall in love with themselves and nature again."

"Weren't you... scared?" said Drew. "That fucking... thing... it's repulsive."

"I feared for my life, for my sanity. For everything. And I didn't believe what I was seeing either... I definitely considered that I was losing my mind, like my dad."

"What did it ask you to do?"

"It said..." Robert's face fell. "It said that it could teach me to paint in a way that everyone would understand... a universal way to create."

Drew remembered seeing Robert Frost painting with his thumbs, mayonnaise, hair, soot, tissue, candle wax, flower petals... anything and everything was a paintbrush or material to create his landscapes. He made it look easy, and it was.

"When did you realise it was using you? From the beginning? When you got your own show? When? Because it was using you, and it has been ever since."

Robert Frost shook his head, suddenly tripping over his words. "I... I don't know... I have no way of knowing... if, by teaching its method to CNN viewers... it could get into people's homes through the art they created. I... I don't know. How does anyone really know the impact they have on others?"

Drew stood over him, his hand slowly moving up to his inside pocket. "But you had a feeling, didn't you? You know... I read an interview you gave in *Splash.* You said you would never sell your paintings because art isn't commerce. It wasn't because you didn't believe in selling art... It's because you knew that if you sold your work, you would give it direct access to other people's homes." Drew leant into Robert Frost, inhaling decades of dry skin and sour sweat. "You made that choice because you already knew it was dangerous. It had already killed, hadn't he?"

"No!" snapped Robert Frost. "Not at the start. I didn't know."

"Then when!" shouted Drew, withdrawing the kitchen knife. "Tell me, or... i'll stab you."

Robert Frost looked up at him, and Drew saw fear in his eyes for the first time. "My wife... I never told her what I knew. But eventually, I couldn't hide from her any more. I told her... and, bless her, she believed me." A tear ran down his cheek, leaving a yellow trail in the grime. "She told me to burn them... the paintings, all of them."

Drew's heart was pounding, sweat pooling around the knife's hilt.

"I said no, and... she let it be. But a few nights later, I found her... late at night, setting a bonfire. I tried to stop her, but she started throwing them in, and... then it came. And..."

"And it killed her."

"Yes..." cried Robert Frost. "My love."

Drew lowered the knife. "Whatever it is... it never cared about people. It never cared about you, art, or any of it. It needed you to spread it around the world, and when she tried to stop it... it punished you."

Robert Frost wept. "I've never told a soul."

Drew grabbed him by the shoulder. "But you got out from under it! How? What deal did you make to save your skin?" Whatever it was, Drew knew it had cost Frost everything. He was an old man living in a cave in the creek with nothing but regrets.

"I... I... I..."

Drew shook him.

"What about the painting? The one in the dining room. That figure wrapped in darkness... Your final painting."

Frost's expression clouded over. "What?"

"Don't play dumb now..." Drew grabbed him by the hair. "How did you get rid of that thing?"

Frost fell to his knees, the white embers puffing a cloud of dust. "I don't know what you mean... It let me live so long as I never told a soul. So long as... I left everything behind and never interfered."

"You're a fucking coward. A coward in a cave... you're a liar!" shouted Drew. His mind was spinning; none of it made sense. "It's still killing."

Frost grabbed his jacket. "The only thing I can think of is... the world changed...something happened... a new way for it to... spread. Maybe... maybe it found someone else to..."

Those words slid into Drew's heart and twisted. They seemed, without definition, to confirm a fear that he hadn't yet been able to give a face. He'd wondered why Ryan hadn't told him about their plans to steal Frost's art and why Charlotte had been so eager to back up the idea that they planned this trip as a surprise for his benefit alone. He didn't know whether it was because he thought so little of himself or because he was intuitive, but he never believed Charlotte booked the lodge based on a memory they both treasured: eating breakfast at her parents' table and watching Frost.

He turned to Charlotte, the kitchen knife glowing orange and red from the embers. "Charlotte... I need you to be honest with me." He walked towards her. "I've had a horrible thought, and I need you to tell me it's not true."

Her eyes filled with tears. She backed away.

"You're not..." he screwed up his face, trying to hold it together. "You're not part of this, are you?"

"Drew... put the knife down." She stepped back into the shadow of the cave.

"I'm not going to hurt you, but you have to tell me," he said, following her.

"Drew, don't..." It sounded like a warning, but he didn't listen.

"It's easy... just... just say it's not true. Tell me you didn't know."

"She knew." Robert Frost was standing by the fire, blocking out the moonlight.

"What?" Ryan didn't know who to face. "Charlotte?" He reached out, groping in the dark to find her. "Why did he say that? Why did he say you knew?" Drew grabbed Charlotte's arm and yanked her out of the shadows. "No! It can't be true!"

A yellow torso, ridged with tiny ribs, appeared before him. Drew looked down. The arm he was holding wasn't Charlotte's; it was shrivelled and greasy and long.

"Oh my..." Frost choked. "Get away!"

A yellow skull plunged out of the gloom and collided with Drew's head with a crack. He fell onto the rocky floor as the cave spun around him.

"No... don't hurt him..." came Charlotte's muffled voice.

A figure loomed over him, breathing. Drew held his hand up in self-defence, but even in his stupor, he knew it was useless.

"Charlotte... please..."

It stamped on his head, and the cave went black.

9

Relief swept through Charlotte as she watched her mom leave. She tottered down the drive, her black dress pegged tightly around her knees and a Dior saddlebag tucked under her armpit. A luxury car with tinted windows waited for her, off to another city function to be gawped at by far less successful men.

Charlotte felt suffocated when her mom was in the house, which she rarely was. If she wasn't having meetings or drafting dinner speeches in her home office, she was knocking on Charlotte's bedroom, asking about homework, grades, weekend jobs, exercise, and whether she was eating healthy. It made Charlotte feel more like a Frankenstein's monster of achievements or failures-in-waiting than a teenager about to start her new life.

Her mom, the CEO of a top New York advertising agency, was a tough act to follow, and Charlotte felt the pressure of it every morning when she woke up before class. She was proud of her mom, but she resented being measured against her, and she feared what would happen if she admitted she wanted the opposite in life. No free cars, client lunches, board meetings or business trips to London: Charlotte wanted to be an artist. How cliché, she thought. The daughter of a successful family turned angsty painter.

Their house was a double-fronted suburban mansion with manicured gardens, five bedrooms, six bathrooms, an indoor hot tub, and a cinema lounge. Her private school friends revelled in its opulence, but she pulled her hood up when she walked up the drive as if the house was a guilty secret.

Once her mom's taxi had disappeared up the street, she ran to her room and pulled out the chest-on-wheels from under her bed that contained all her art supplies. The twice-weekly cleaner ensured her room was spotless, but Charlotte's art chest was gloriously chaotic. She was working on a self-portrait, an exercise in turning herself inside-out, wearing all her insecurities on her skin. It wasn't flattering; her face was acne-scarred, her lips cracked, and the colour of wilting rose petals.

She lay a bed sheet on the floor and began squirting oil paint onto a pallet caked with layers of colour. Sticking her thumb into a purple-blue dollop, she dabbed her self-portrait's chest with paint, creating bruises. She'd adapted this technique from watching Robert Frost, TV's P.I.Y. sensation. His paintings were corny, but the way he turned the ordinary into the extraordinary was magnetic. There was something deeply personal about painting using the body: a fingernail gouge here and a palm smear there. She wanted to leave as much of herself on the canvas as possible, and without any formal art training, every stroke and splatter was a rebellion. Hours would go by when she was painting. Even when her stomach grumbled and her bladder ached, she wouldn't stop, the sun's shadows sliding across the wall until her room was dark.

All she had left was to add the final and most important element: The eyes. If Charlotte was being honest, the eyes were her Achilles heel. Bringing them to life was tricky;

they had a way of changing the entire feel of a painting if they were a millimetre out or a shade too light. She sat back and wondered what she wanted the eyes to say. If, as was popularly thought, they were the windows to the soul, then she wondered what kind of soul she had. It was a question she was scared to ask herself because the answer made her want to cry. Charlotte didn't know who she was outside this room and worried that she was nothing without paint smeared across her hand.

Nothing. That's what she needed to convey.

Placing her index and middle finger on top of the two blank spaces where her eyes would go, she pressed as hard as she could until she heard the canvas rip. "Ahh!" One of her nails had snagged on the canvas strands and ripped out the cuticle. Blood dripped onto the self-portrait before she could suck it clean. She wrapped her finger in a tissue and looked at the bright red splotch that had fallen on the crest of her lip. For some reason, it made sense. She'd let it dry dark.

The doorbell rang.

That would be Ryan and Drew, her two oldest friends. Charlotte's house was the main hangout because her mom was always away. They'd drink tequila, eat junk food and watch horror movies in the cinema lounge, same as always. She didn't like the thought of them splitting up. College was just around the corner; Ryan would be off to business school, Drew to computer science, and she... well, her mom still believed she wanted to study history at Yale.

Propping the painting against the wall, she ran down the stairs barefoot and opened the door. Ryan had Drew in a headlock, dragging his knuckles through his dark hair.

"For fuck sake, Ryan," she said, pulling him away.

Drew shook himself off and smoothed down his hair into a Justin Beiber flick that he was always trying to perfect, but his hair was too wiry to play nice.

"Hey, Charlotte," said Ryan, fist-bumping her.

"Hey," said Drew, giving her a cagey hug. He smelt of sweat and boy's deodorant. "What happened to your finger?"

"Oh… nothing. I was painting and…"

"When you gonna let us see that shit!" said Ryan, divebombing onto the couch.

Charlotte blushed. "Someday."

"You'll never be a real artist until you show people the goods. What's the point otherwise?" said Ryan.

Drew shook his head at that and blinked reassuringly. Charlotte didn't expect Ryan to understand; he was a cultural Neanderthal, but Drew was sensitive; he played the guitar and taught himself to code, which was creative in her eyes.

"What are we watching tonight? I vote something disgusting," said Ryan.

"Well… are you talking Braindead or Hostel? Funny-gore or disturbing-gore?" she said, heading for her mum's liquor cabinet, which was never understocked.

"Disturbing gore!" said Drew and Ryan together before laughing.

"But not Hostel, I've seen it twice. How about…"

"No. We are not watching a Serbian Film."

Ryan punched a pillow. "Dammit!"

"You ask every single time, and I say… I don't want that showing up on my mum's bill," she giggled, sloshing tequila into plastic cups.

"How about… The Human Centipede," he came back.

"That's kinda funny gore, isn't it?" said Drew.

"I mean… the concept is hilarious, but apparently it's sickening."

"I think it's kinda hot," said Ryan, winking at Charlotte before taking a huge gulp. "Ahhh! Delicious."

"Gross," she said. "But sure…"

"Haha… butt."

She threw a pillow at him. Ryan might have been a

total idiot, but there was something charming about how filterless he was. Drew was shy and thoughtful, which was adorable, but he was afraid to spread out and take up space. Ryan would run through the house naked if he could. Part of her wanted him to.

"Pizza?" said Drew.

"Where would you want to be in the centipede line-up?" interrupted Ryan. "Out of the three of us?"

"Ryan…" said Drew, rolling his eyes.

"I mean… is that even a question? The front, obviously," Charlotte replied.

"So you'd like to shit in my mouth," he winked.

Drew choked.

"Fucking… Ew," she covered her face. "Anyway… who said it'd be your mouth…" she said, looking at Drew.

"Charlotte! No!" Drew whined.

"I'd go at the back," said Ryan, "I wouldn't want to shit in either of your mouths."

"How very selfless," she said, picking up the TV remote.

"Pizza?" repeated Drew, louder this time.

"With Meatballs, please," said Ryan before Charlotte chased him off the couch.

Pizza, it turned out, was the wrong choice when watching a movie about a mad scientist sewing mouths and assholes. Ryan kept being disgusting and stretching the cheese with his lips while Drew and Charlotte dry heaved in the corner. She would miss them next year, but she knew they'd make the effort to stay in touch. Drew was basically in love with her, which she felt like a dick for thinking to herself, and Ryan's house parties would be unmissable. When all was said and done, they were like family to her, and she was incredibly thankful for their companionship.

"I'm kinda tipsy," she said, swaying by the TV.

"Same," said Drew, his eyes closing.

"You guys are weak sauce." Ryan bounced off the couch and went down on one knee, "Charlotte… my dear, will you marry me?"

Charlotte snorted and shoved him in the forehead. "You're definitely drunk." She yawned. "Mom's gonna be back soon; you guys should head off."

"Ohhh," pleaded Ryan, pulling a puppy-eyed face. "Can't I crash here? Not Drew… he's too stinky."

"Hey, no…" said Charlotte, her face tightening. "Don't be mean." She looked at Drew and immediately regretted coming to his defence as if, in some way, it had legitimised Ryan's dig. "And no. You can't. I have to get up early tomorrow. Doctor's appointment."

"Fine!" flounced Ryan, "Stinky will have to do," he said, leaping on Drew and humping the side of his thigh.

"Jesus, man… fuck off!" Drew pushed Ryan away and accidentally elbowed him in the jaw.

"Alright, alright…" chuckled Ryan with tears in his eyes from the knock. He knew when he'd crossed a line. Drew was trying not to look hurt.

Charlotte showed them out. Ryan held on to her for too long, and she had to force him away with a giggle.

"Everything okay?" said Drew from beneath his fringe.

"Yeah?"

"I mean with the doctor's appointment."

"Oh… It's nothing. Just a check-up."

He nodded. "I'd really like to see the painting you've been working on. I'm sure it's great."

"Thanks," she shrugged, "It's actually… not too bad."

"I bet," he said, going in for a hug and accidentally nudging one of her breasts. He froze.

"Jeez, Drew, anyone would think you hitting me in the face and touching Charlotte's boob was intentional," jeered Ryan from the path.

"Sorry…" Drew said, stepping back.

"Don't be… it's just a boob," she said. "Honestly, it's fine." He couldn't meet her eye.

"Come on, bro, before you accidentally grab her…"

whistled Ryan.

Charlotte fist-bumped Drew's chest. "Now we're even... Sleep well, man."

"Thanks... you too. And thanks for the pizza... actually, I don't think I ate any," he said.

She watched them leave and closed the door. She'd lied. Her mom wouldn't be back until midnight, but she wanted a couple of hours alone to enjoy her finished self-portrait. Charlotte scampered up the stairs and into the dark of her bedroom, which smelt of sticky oil paint. Her painting, an eyeless girl with livid skin, sat waiting for her next to the head of her bed. It still looked good, she thought with a sigh. The drop of blood had turned brown and dribbled from the bottom lip onto her chin; a nice touch.

She wanted to hang it on her wall, but that would mean her mom would see it, inviting criticism and possibly disgust. Charlotte wanted to be praised by her mom more than anything. She resented that power and the fact her mom didn't seem to know or care that she had it. Worst of all, she feared that her mom might never notice.

"Screw it," she said, going to a drawer and rummaging around for a loose nail. She was doing this for herself.

The walls vibrated as she slammed the sole of her Doc Martin boots against the nail, driving it deep. She picked up the painting and hung it. It was an explosion of colour against the creme wallpaper, a real fuck-you to the oppressively bland suburban palette. Charlotte stared at the girl with torn eyes and a bruised chest, and something swelled in her chest—not pride, not pity, but desire. Desire to fill all the walls with colour, not eke out tiny squares for herself. But as much as she wanted to rebel, she didn't want to alienate herself from her mom. As much as she desired freedom, she desired acceptance.

She downed a few more gulps of Tequila and filled the last few inches of the bottle with water to cover her tracks. She had to be up in the morning for the appointment, and her mom would be pissed if she wasn't asleep when she got back. Charlotte stripped off and climbed under her duvet, feeling the liquor blazing through her veins. She understood why people became alcoholics; it burnt the pain away.

The next thing she knew, someone was in the room with her.

"Hey, Charlotte," her mom was sitting on the end of her bed in the dark.

"Mom? What..." She must have fallen asleep.

"Sorry for waking you," she said, sounding tipsy. "I just put my head in to see if you were okay, and... I saw that you've put something on your wall. It's... Did you make it?"

"Can we do this in the morning?" mumbled Charlotte, still half asleep.

Her mom stood up and walked towards the painting.

"I think we need to talk..." She sounded tired.

Charlotte looked at her alarm clock. "Mom... It's 01:00 AM... I have that appointment."

"Yes... Better safe than sorry. It runs in the family, you know..." She set her Dior handbag down on the bed, the hot smell of red wine breath wafting through the air.

Charlotte reached for the night light.

"No... don't, I've got a headache," said her mom. "Too much wine. The dark is nice."

Charlotte reached for her glasses and put them on. It was still too dark to see, but she could make out her mum's outline against the drapes, tall and a little hunched.

"You know... I think you've got something here. It's very... passionate."

"Mom, you can't even see it properly. Can't we wait until tomorrow?"

Her mom reached down towards Charlotte and stroked her hair with slender fingers, cold from the outside air. "I know I can be tough on you... I just... I had a big meeting today that didn't go how I wanted. Hundreds of hours of planning. Poof." Her mum's fingers unfurled.

"I'm sorry," said Charlotte, dragging herself up the headboard.

"I guess..." Her mom's S's slurred into H's. "It's not all about how much work you put into something... things don't always work out. But... this... this is good," she said, pointing at the painting. "This looks like it comes easy. I think... I think I can help you with this. There's potential."

Charlotte didn't believe what she was hearing. The idea that all it took to get her mom's attention was to hang a painting on the wall was infuriating and embarrassing. She'd tried to talk to her several times about art, but she'd never shown any interest before now. Maybe it was the wine and the self-pity of losing a client talking.

"I think I can help," she repeated, her voice dropping an octave and cracking back up to its normal pitch.

"What do you mean help?"

"Oh... I know people. There's a guy who does graphics for us sometimes. A genius... I think he's called Beetle... or something. He does digital art. It's gonna be big... in the art scene. Lots of eyeballs out there... the internet..."

Her mom stroked the painting, her long fingers reaching the eye holes.

"It's so sad, though." Her mom's jaw distended down in a yawn but made no sound.

"Mum... I appreciate it, I really do, but let's talk over breakfast, yeah? I'd like that. A lot."

"Sure... sure..." she said, "I won't forget."

Charlotte's mother bent down and kissed her roughly on the forehead, her dark hair hanging over her face. When she pulled away, the smell of leaves followed her. "Sleep well, Charlie," she said in a low whisper.

"You too..." said Charlotte. The room felt odd.

Her mom walked across the room on tiptoes and out of the room.

"That was fucking weird," said Charlotte aloud,

muffling a smile. She'd waited a long time to hear those words. It didn't matter that she was drunk, just as long as she remembered in the morning.

Charlotte turned onto her side, looking up at the dimly lit portrait. It did look good; anyone could see that. Those eyes— so much depth. The skin was almost yellow from the streetlamps outside, and the texture of the oil paint crusted off the canvas in such a realistic way.

"She's right, you know," a voice, thick as mud, spoke through the painting's bloody lips. "You could go far."

Outside, she heard the sound of Mom unlocking the front door.

10

When Drew woke up, he found himself tied to one of the chairs in the dining room at Frost's Lodge. Two Charlottes and two Frosts were also tied up next to him; his vision doubled, almost certainly concussed. Whenever he moved his head, nausea grinned in the pit of his stomach.

"What's happening?" said Drew, spittle swinging from his lips. Charlotte stared at the table, her skin pale, purple folds hanging under her eyes. Drew twisted his wrists, and the ropes croaked. "Charlotte... what the fuck..."

The black cloak covering Frost's final painting began to bulge. Frost moaned and tried to move away from the growing shape, but his legs were tied to the chair.

"What do we do!" Drew bucked, the legs of his chairs jumping an inch and almost toppling backwards. Acid burned in his throat. "Charlotte!"

"I didn't mean to..." she whispered.

A tall figure emerged from the painting and stood at the end of the table, shrouded in the black cloak. It breathed hungrily, every inhalation sucking the fabric into its mouth.

"What the…"

"Don't talk to it!" Shouted Frost, twisting his head around. The creature's hands shot from underneath its cloak, reaching around Frost's body and grabbing him by the ribcage. The old man squealed as its yellow hands gripped the bottom of his ribs and began to prize them upwards. Frost's shirt ripped open, revealing soft, wrinkled skin that started to stretch in red smiles as his blood vessels burst.

"Please! Stop!" he cried, but the creature wouldn't. His skin unzipped in a single fluid line. Drew saw yellow fat behind it, grey organs and a fuzz of bloody veins all jiggling in his chest. Frost's sternum cracked, and his ribcage flew apart like wings. Drew spewed a jet of clear liquid puke across the table.

The creature began to dip its hands into Frost's chest like needles in an industrial sewing machine. It flung the slop from its fingers onto the wall and began to smear, using Frost's blood and guts as paint. The more meat it slapped on, the more the wall seemed to deform, shimmering and swirling in a riot of gore. A shaft of red light burst through the mess.

Drew's soul gagged. It seemed as if the creature had painted a portal directly into Frost's mind, his memories flashing through the wall in bursts of red light: a stormy ocean, pine woods, trash-ridden cities, TV studios, stuffy offices and dive bars, all flickering next, next, next like a slideshow.

The creature spoke with its back to them as it worked. "Look, see," its voice reverberated. "I can take you anywhere, make you feel anything you want; I paint dreams. I paint realities."

"Charlotte!" Drew shouted.

Charlotte's head was cricked against the table, her face twisted in fear and amazement. Robert Frost had turned entirely white; all the colour busted out of his chest.

"I'm sorry," murmured Charlotte.

"What do we do?" Drew strained against his binds and instantly felt light-headed.

The creature's arm extended across the dining room and grabbed Drew by the throat, lifting him into the air, chair and all. As he tilted, the carving knife fell from his inside pocket, pinging across the floor and landing a few feet from Charlotte on the tabletop.

The creature held him up to its creation, showing him what it had made. Drew was looking through the wall now, a thousand images shining through the blood-smeared window. It was awesome and horrific.

"What... are you?" choked Drew.

Its teeth chattered beneath its hood. "I am... The Artist."

Drew squeezed his eyes shut, but the creature stretched them open again.

"I can take the pain away. I want to take everyone's pain away. Let me, please." It pushed Drew's face into the slop, and he felt his cheeks hum with an electric charge. "You don't have to be afraid anymore; look... I'll show you." With that, it melted through the window it had made and vanished, dropping Drew. Drew landed on his shoulder, which exploded under the weight of his body.

He groaned. "Charlotte... the knife. Knock it down to me..."

Whatever reason The Artist had for leaving alone, he knew it wouldn't be for long. "Charlotte, you fucking... why is this happening? Why did you do this?"

"He came to me. He said that... he could help me connect with my mom... that I could make her proud." Her voice was monotone. "He said he could make me a world-famous artist..."

Drew tried to squeeze his hands through the knots, but they were too tight. "You too? The same bullshit as Frost?" Drew jerked his head at Frost. "You just... accepted it? From that thing… that unnatural thing?"

Charlotte pushed away from the table, the chair legs howling against the wooden floor. Her eyes were black. "Don't you think I know? Don't you think I know how fucking stupid and… twisted… and crazy…"

Drew spat at her, but it missed and he watched the gloop slide off the table's edge.

"I deserve that and worse…"

"I… loved you…" stammered Drew.

"I was miserable. Nothing was ever good enough for my mom; you knew how she could be. She'd loosen up after a few red wines, but that wasn't the real her… she was cruel…"

"Both my parents are gone! You don't see me making deals with the devil!" cried Drew.

Charlotte's gaze hardened. "You'd do anything to get close to them again." She lowered her voice and gestured to the kitchen. "It… is unbelievable. You have no idea how much power…"

"I don't care about power, Charlotte…" Drew began to cry. "I just want to live… get the knife and help me…"

"No… listen to me. It can help you… you're parents…"

Drew felt a surge of white-hot hate so pure he thought it would beam through his skin and melt her like magma. "Don't you… you fuckin' spoilt… piece of shit… I earned my life. I fought for my little piece… against everything that's been thrown at me. So don't flaunt you're… evil… like it's hope. We're not the same… I thought we were… but I'm nothing like you."

She fixed him with a dead-eyed stare. "It said it'd kill me… if I didn't help it," she inhaled. "It said… it'd kill me and everyone I loved… that means you."

"Well, it looks like it got it both ways." He craned his neck towards her. "Grey… Ryan?"

"I didn't know."

"Bullshit! You were trying to save your skin… from

whatever mess you got into. You did this!"

"No!" Charlotte's chest pumped. "No..."

Drew searched for pity, but his heart was a desert, dry of empathy, another thing Charlotte had stolen from him. "You selfish fucking..." muttered Drew. He looked up at her, tears magnifying his eyes. He didn't want to believe the thoughts that squirmed inside his head, the things he was scared he had known all along.

"You're the reason we're here, aren't you? Just say it. Say it before that thing paints me onto the fucking wall." Drew suddenly knew why he had felt so empty the past few years, why he felt so lost, wondering how he'd ended up staring at screens all day, selling pixels to incels. That wasn't who he wanted to be. Now he knew it was because she manipulated him into it, used his love against him, to serve her master. "You should have said no. You... both you and Frost... knew that it was evil, but you made a deal with it anyway. I would have rather died..." said Drew.

Charlotte bit the top of her shirt and dragged it up, exposing her belly. There was a purple lump protruding from her abdomen. "Well, I can't! I can't just... die."

Drew craned his neck up. "What... what the fuck is that?"

She shook her head, tears running down her cheeks. "Oh, Drew... I'm sorry... I wanted to tell... I'm... I'm... dying."

Drew's brain shrivelled up and crawled down his spine.

11

"**C**harlotte... Grey! It's time!" Charlotte heard Ryan calling from downstairs. The moment she had dreaded had arrived.

"He's right. It's time," said a shadow in the corner of the room. "You've done a wonderful job... you're a true artist."

Charlotte pulled off her paint-stained top and threw it on the bed. The tumour in her stomach stared at her.

"It's advanced. Not long now." The shadow stepped into the light, yellow forearms hanging by its skinny waist.

"I do this... and you'll bring me back. That's the deal."

The figure made a noise that sounded like dry leaves being crushed. Charlotte took it as confirmation.

"Drew saw the paint on my top... did you do that?" she said, quickly applying black eyeliner in the mirror.

"To remind you..."

"Of what? You'll leave them out of it. This is between you and me," she said.

"As long as you hold up your end, I will mine."

Charlotte didn't want to die. She still hadn't found a way to connect with her mom, and she definitely hadn't made it as a painter the way The Artist had promised her. She was too young to go, and she felt within her rights to do anything she could to stop her final day from coming.

Charlotte slammed the door and ran to the dining room where Ryan was preparing for his big speech. Drew smiled at her bashfully and complimented her makeup, which made her feel sick.

Her painting stood at the back of the dining room, covered by a black cloth. Frost was probably the easiest artist to forge because he had broadcast his method on national television for the better part of two decades, but she'd decided to add her own touch to this one. It needed to be ugly and terrifying to sell the mystique. The plan had worked. Charlotte knew Ryan could not resist something as dramatic as this: a story about a famous artist who lost his mind and vanished into the wilderness after painting his final vision. The fact that Frost never copyrighted his work was a coincidence. They would turn Frost's paintings into digital art, spreading The Artist's influence to unsuspecting crypto bros across the world.

Ryan's speech went off without a hitch, although she could tell Drew was suspicious. She'd expected that, which is why she'd planned to tell him about the tumour that was growing on her liver the following morning when Ryan was too hungover to care. She knew that by anyone else's standards, snorting cocaine when her body was shutting down was bordering on suicide, but she'd made a deal with The Artist, and if it came through, she wouldn't have to worry about her body ever again.

That night, Ryan got so high that he decided to bring forward the launch of Frost's NFT collection. "I just think we should do it tonight. Why wait? I mean, we've got the investors lined up, and the Madwire update is going live in the morning. What's stopping us?"

Charlotte didn't protest. The sooner she satisfied The Artist, the sooner they could conclude their deal. She knew she was being selfish, but she thought selflessness was reserved for those who weren't staring into the abyss.

After they'd photographed and uploaded Frost's artwork to Totem, Ryan wanted to fuck. Charlotte said no. The tumour was a good excuse. He knew about it, of course, but she hadn't told him the whole truth; she'd said it was benign. He was too self-absorbed to question it, which was part of why they couldn't be together. She didn't want a partner who took her word as gospel.

The following day, she found Drew looking sad on the porch. He'd lost both his parents to cancer, which meant she knew the news would devastate him. Charlotte knew how much he cared about her and that if she came clean, his care would eclipse Ryan's. She understood the power she had over him. He was a red-breasted robin in her hand; she could crush him with one squeeze.

Robert Frost's story differed from hers, but wherever he'd ended up, it was for the same reasons. She was horrified when she saw him watching them from behind the rocks, so skinny and dried out. Drew had thought it was an animal, and as chance would have it, a White Deer appeared to indulge his theory. She'd fed him enough truth to keep his eye off the ball; she knew he would be drunk on the idea that she was leaving Ryan.

None of this meant that she didn't hate herself for what she was doing. She knew The Artist lived off pain and death; without it, he had no purpose, and she was part of his plan. Charlotte didn't care about the idiots who paid thousands for Totem's pixel art, but she also didn't want to be responsible for The Artist finding their way to them. So, she came up with a plan.

The doctors had given her three months to live six months ago, which meant she was on borrowed time. The deal she'd made with The Artist was that, in return for allowing him to use Frost's NFT collection as a vessel to exploit their collectors, it would bring her back from the dead. Grey was the main developer and engineer, the only one of the four with the skill to sabotage the launch of Frost's digital collection. She needed to convince him to delete the collection post-launch, which was fraudulent and against Grey's principles as a true believer in the platform they had built. She knew she couldn't tell him the truth, that The Artist had possessed Frost's art and would be able to use it as a portal into people's lives; that sounded insane, so she came up with a reasonable excuse.

When she returned from her walk with Drew, she cornered him in the bathroom. "Grey... we fucked up."

"What?" He looked scared.

"The collection... I just got a notice from NBC's lawyers. They are claiming ownership of Robert Frost's art, that, as they paid for his show, Easy as PIY, and his work was created on their time, they are entitled to be involved with any sale of his work." Charlotte stripped off quickly with her back to him, showing him enough flesh to make him nervous but not enough that he would see her weakness. She slipped into the bath. "I'm not sure if it's bullshit yet. But I think we should refund the investors and freeze the collection. We don't have the firepower to go up against NBC."

"That's... not how it works. It's out of our hands now."

"I know, but... if we make our investors whole again and put the project on ice, then no one is losing. Sure, our treasury takes a hit, but... that's better than bankruptcy. You don't want forensic accountants looking through your accounts, do you?"

Charlotte had to suffocate the voice in her head that told her she was a terrible person for manipulating her friend. She was doing this for the right reasons, trying to save people's lives.

"Um... I mean... I'll have to think about it."

"No rush, I can hold them off for a while... but don't say anything to Ryan or Drew. They'll freak."

Grey nodded. She didn't know if he'd come through for her, but at least she'd tried. Grey looked happy to escape, but as he left, he ran into Ryan and Drew, who seemed worked up. Ryan barged in, babbling something about a painting involving Grey. When it dawned on her, it took everything she had not to shit out her heart. The Artist must have heard her telling Grey to sabotage the collection. She didn't know how it had worked so quickly, but when she saw the painting of Ryan overlooking a field of sheep, she knew what it was: An omen, just as Drew had said.

Fucking Drew.

Charlotte instantly realised that her plan was nothing more than a rope bridge made of rotting planks, the abyss waiting below to swallow her up. The same selfishness that had driven her to take The Artist up on its deal was the same selfishness that had condemned her friends. It shouldn't have come as a surprise, but the shock of realising how little control she had made her want to throw herself out of Drew's window.

The Artist had been listening to her thoughts.

Grey's death was swift and punishing. As she watched him lying broken on the porch roof, she knew an evil far worse than the tumour feasting on her tissue had infected her. She was the least close to Grey of the four, but he was part of their gang, and she knew it was her fault. The guilt clung to her back like a giant spider.

"Tch-tch-tch," tutted The Artist when Ryan and Drew searched the lodge to find Grey's killer. "I told you that your friends would pay if you weren't careful. You've only got yourself to blame."

"I... didn't..."

"No, of course not. But don't worry, he doesn't have any pain anymore. I'll paint a lovely picture with his blood and send him to his peace."

"But... how?"

The Artist stood behind her, breathing. "There's a

universe in everyone, and I hold the keys."

"What's the key?"

"The key is understanding that humans long for connection." It placed its yellow fingers on her shoulder. "Drew only learnt to play the guitar so you would notice him, you only painted so your mum could see you were more than just her daughter, and Frost only painted the creek because he wanted to feel part of the golden hour, for once, he wanted to be beautiful. The only function of art, no matter what anybody says, is to stop people from feeling alone. When I paint with them, I make them truly beautiful. I connect them to themselves so they are not alone anymore. Once I close the circuit, they live on eternally."

Its words were sickly poison. When The Artist said it helped take people's pain away, she knew it meant killing.

"I don't believe you."

It patted her head. "You will, soon enough."

She felt it start to fade. "Can't you bring Grey back?"

The Artist froze. "Are you willing to exchange your life for his?"

She didn't answer.

"I thought not."

So, just as she had tried to sabotage The Artist, it sabotaged her, sending her and her friends into the woods in a tailspin of fear, anger and confusion. When Frost found her, or as he thought, saved her, she was considering ending it all. She didn't struggle when he pulled her away from Ryan and Drew, fused in a bloody pile. She knew that The Artist would keep its word, and if she never got what she bargained for, eternal life, it wouldn't matter. Nothingness would suffice.

12

Drew stared at her. Between the bloody wall, pulsing light and Charlotte, his lost love, admitting she had made a necromantic pact to save herself from a terminal illness, he tasted, for the first time since his parents died, how profoundly shit life was. Bile coated his throat. He wished he could choke on it. "I... I don't know what to say."

"I'm sorry," she said. "I never believed... I never thought anything like this could happen."

Drew never believed his parents would die before he turned thirty, but that illusion had its neck snapped without much struggle. "You could have said something," he sniffed.

"At first, it coached me in painting beautiful things that people would want to own... a piece of me. Years went by, and I didn't hear from it... but I felt it staring at me through my work and saw its eyes in every gallery I visited. I thought I was... cursed." Her eyes fell. "Can you imagine? The paranoia, always wondering if it was real... if it really was me pulling the strings, or it... if I'd told anyone, I'd have been locked up."

"You should have been," said Drew.

"I disagree," came The Artist's voice. It was still cloaked in black, but it carried something over its shoulder. "If she had been locked up, then she would never have been given the chance to..." He tossed his load onto the table. "Truly... live."

Robert Frost lay on the table shivering, the light from the fleshy portal flashing across him and his exploded corpse sitting at the opposite end. Drew let out a cry and forced his way along the wall. The living Frost looked at him with bemused curiosity.

"See, Charlotte, I mean what I say," said The Artist. "I brought him back."

"What the fuck!" yelled Drew.

"Don't be frightened," said The Artist, plucking Charlotte up and unwrapping the ropes which bound her hands. "In my art, I create universes where we can live forever, free from pain. That means you, too, Drew. All you have to do is tell me what you desire, and I will show you." It held her in its long, yellow arms and stroked her hair. "You deserve to feel love. You've earned it," it said, kissing her forehead through the black sheet. "You did what I asked, so... let me show you."

Charlotte heaved the knife between its ribs. The Artist inhaled, sucking a twist of black fabric down its throat. It writhed backwards through the room.

"Quickly," said Charlotte, falling towards Drew and hacking at the ropes.

Pain radiated through Drew's body, fusing his joints at the hinges. "Fuck!" he grimaced, holding his dead arm. The last bind snapped free, and Charlotte grabbed his hand and pulled him up. Drew stumbled up as The Artist flailed around the dining room, its bony arms smashing and cracking against the table.

"To the creek!" She shouted. This was the only chance they'd have, so they ran.

The sun was coming up through the trees when they crashed through the wreckage of the porch and down the path towards the lake. Drew could hear The Artist's long strides following, galloping over the dead leaves and swinging through the trees.

"Don't look back," he cried.

They were about to reach the banks of the lake when The Artist's footsteps stopped thudding, and an uneasy quiet filled the air.

"To the right!" called Charlotte.

A shadow enveloped her, and The Artist, who had leapt into a dive, grappled her into the water. The Artist's legs wrapped around her torso, spinning her in a death roll, its black sockets bursting out of the water and then disappearing in a blur. Drew threw himself in after them, but the cold water took his breath away, and he began to panic. Charlotte didn't scream. All he could hear was the sound of the golden lake churning.

"I'll make a deal with you! Just... please stop. I want you to take my pain away!"

Their bodies drifted below.

Drew fell to his knees in prayer. "I need you to take this pain away."

The Artist rose from the lake, its cloak gone, brown water slipping between its teeth and down its shining yellow skin. "That's all I want," It said. "I want to take your pain away forever."

Charlotte's body bobbed to the surface.

"That's why you're the greatest artist," nodded Drew.

The Artist smiled. "How can I help you?"

Drew looked at Charlotte, floating face down, her brown hair parted like The Artist's fingers. "I want... I want her. I want her to live," he said, pointing.

The Artist's smile looked like a split tree, with jagged teeth and raw bones. "Ah, love. The greatest work of art."

Drew stood still, his dislocated shoulder swinging.

"What do I have to give you for her?"

The Artist walked towards him, cupping his chin with its long, paintbrush fingers.

"I want to take the pain away. Will you let me do that when all is said and done?" Its voice was soft.

"Yes." And Drew meant it.

Keeping its hollow eyes on Drew, it reached back and dragged Charlotte out of the water. Her lips were blue, and one of her eyes was half open.

"Is she... is she alive?"

It stared at him. "If you want her to be."

Drew felt his blood go runny. "I've loved her forever... since I first saw her..."

It held its hand up. "First. I know you work with computers. Code."

Drew stiffened. He didn't confirm or deny it.

"I want to learn this," it said. "Will you help me?" It reached out and gripped Drew under the chin, its face still.

Drew knew at that moment that if he said no, both he and Charlotte would die. He thought about how much he had hated her back in the dining room, the betrayal and the lies. Now that he was faced with the same dilemma, to resurrect her, he regretted what he had said. He couldn't blame her for trying to grasp life before it slipped away forever. That was natural, only human and, after all, the pursuit of art was only ever about immortalising something fleeting: a sunset... love.

"I've done books, paintings, film, music, sculpture..." It said.

"No." Drew shook his head. "I won't help you. I can't... it's just... I can't. It's not worth it... I wish it were... but I couldn't live with myself."

A jellyfish tongue flopped between its gristly lips. "I admire your honesty." Its grip tightened. "There are many others."

The muscles in Drew's throat twanged as his windpipe

was slowly crushed. He gasped for air as stars filled his eyes. It was dawn, but for Drew, night was falling fast. Charlotte lay on the bank, motionless and pale. Drew savoured the sight of her. Unrequited or not, his heart had always beat for her; if this were it, its last beats would be hers.

The Artist's body snapped in half as something white collided with it. Drew was flung into the water, leaves clogging his open mouth. He rose, sputtering, to see something mounting The Artist—a White Deer. The Artist screamed as the deer gored it, its mossy antler embedded in The Artist's face. The sound The Artist made shook the trees, sending birds flapping and cascading golden leaves into the lake.

Ryan appeared before Drew, lying half-naked on the couch, telling him that White Deers, Bái lù, meant good luck. He hadn't believed him then, but as he watched the deer, its snout smeared with The Artist's yellow blood, a tear rolled down his cheek and fell into the lake. The White Deer grunted and stabbed The Artist's face for a few more seconds before trotting off into the wood, ragged but serene.

Drew splashed out of the lake and grabbed a rock, ready to smash The Artist's face in, but when he reached the carcass, he saw that the deer hadn't left much to finish. The Artist's head was split open, revealing a strangely human pulp of off-white brain. Drew lifted the rock above his head, tears pouring. He had lost everything: Grey, Ryan and now Charlotte.

The Artist's fingers twitched and touched the water, sending a ripple that surfed to the centre of the lake. The golden waters, reflecting the leaves, started to shimmer like the dining room wall covered in Frost's blood, and the clearing was suddenly filled with bright light.

"Drew... son, is that you?" A man and a woman's voices, somehow familiar to his ears but uncanny, like a memory misremembered. "It is you! Come... we've been waiting.

We've missed you."

Drew staggered back from the shore, flitting from The Artist to the lake, its waters plunging like a waterfall. He thought he could see them: Dad with thick white hair and Mum waving in her pink coat. "Please, before it's too late!" They called out, their voices rippling with the lake.

It was probably The Artist's last attempt to lure him towards an inevitable fate, that or a postmortem spasm, the dregs of its evil magic seeping out. Part of him didn't care which it was; it was a dream that tempted him with long, coaxing fingers.

"Mum? Dad?"

"Yes, son, we're here. But hurry."

He waded into the water, the light soaking through him. Maybe, like Frost, it would be best if he vanished into the wilderness for good. At least then, he wouldn't have to explain what had happened in the creek.

They were fading. "Come quick, it's closing."

He sank to his shoulders, the golden waters kissing his chin. "Will you take my hand?" Drew said, reaching down.

No reply came. It was quiet down there in the lake. The water drained into his mouth. It tasted of dirt. It filled his ears. This might be his last chance to choose what kind of life he wanted, to be free finally. No pain. To forget.

As he disappeared below the surface, he thought he heard Charlotte cough.

AFTERWORD

Creativity and art bridges the gap between what we feel and what we can explain... it's a kind of magic. I truly believe this magic is in all of us, whether we know it or not; an impulse to connect and empathise.

Art exists to make us forget, to take our pain away, whether it's a glance at a painting, a three-minute song, or a long book. It's therapy, and it's meant to do good, even if sometimes, the content hurts.

Don't be like The Artist. Don't use that magic in you to further your own ends and put other people down. You can't control how people perceive what you do, but you can control your intention.

However you choose to communicate your magic, do it with love, for yourself and others.

See you next time!

ACKNOWLEDGEMENT

Thank you very much for reading The Artist. This is my first ever self-published novella, and I am deeply touched that you have made it to the end.

To all my lovely Horror BookTok friends... thank you for your support. I wouldn't have written this without your encouragement.

If you liked The Artist, please leave a review and tag me in your social media posts. If you hated it... let me know, too. I'm always open to feedback!

TikTok: @inigohorror
Instagram: @inigohorror

Printed in Dunstable, United Kingdom